JUSTIN'S BODY

OF WORK

JANICE L. DENNIE

KENTE ROMANCE
An Imprint of Kente Publications
P.O. Box 184
Jackson, CA 95642

Copyright © 2015 Janice L. Dennie
ISBN-10: 096433495X
ISBN-13: 9780964334953

Names, characters and incidents depicted in this book are products of the author's imagination, or are used in a fictitious situation. Any resemblances to actual events, locations, organizations, incidents or persons–living or dead–are coincidental and beyond the intent of the author.

JUSTIN'S BODY OF WORK

***

To Gregory D. Reed, Sr. My husband and best friend.

To all of my readers who enjoy reading about the Underwood's of Napa Valley, this book is for you.

Other books by Janice L. Dennie

KENTON'S VINTAGE AFFAIR

Unemployed chef, Briana Rutledge inherits a cottage on one thousand acres of land in California's Napa Valley, making her a millionaire. She sets out to turn the cottage into her dream restaurant. But others have agendas to destroy Briana and her plans.

The Underwood brothers have inherited the character DNA of their male ancestors, a line of old fashioned southern gentlemen who took great pride in protecting women and children. As the eldest brother, Kenton Underwood has been betrayed and no longer believes women need his protection. He has no room for love until he meets sexy, understated, Briana Rutledge, who finds a special place in his heart.

THE LION OF JUDAH

Prince Johannas of Ethiopia is torn apart by the escalating civil war in his country. Knowing a new constitution will end the war, he comes to the United States to finish the precious document. He never expects, however, to meet the woman of his dreams, especially when a deadly accident throws her literally at his feet.

MOON GODDESS QUEEN OF SHEBA

For the first time ever, powerful King Solomon has been conquered, and by the defiant and beautiful Queen of Sheba. He must have the sensuous enchantress who resists his remedy for the alliance she seeks. And he will risk life itself to protect the woman who has pierced his heart with a tender love that he cannot deny.

Dear Reader,

I enjoyed writing Justin Underwood's story. He's a passionate civil rights attorney and a voice for the voiceless and disenfranchised. His body of work consists of arguing women's rights issues involving sexual discrimination, equal pay and domestic abuse cases in court. Although I don't consider myself a hard core feminist, I do appreciate when the people take up a shield to protect human rights.

You may ask, why would I pair Justin with a non-committal spa owner and masseuse like Ashley Jacobs, who has a family secret that keeps her from developing intimate relationships. The fire between Ashley and Justin ignites after Ashley gives Justin the massage of his life.

If this is your first time reading about the Underwood's of Napa Valley, you can read each book as a stand-alone.

Sit back, relax and enjoy reading *Justin's Body of Work*.

Janice

Chapter 1

Ashley Jacobs drove her Mazda convertible in the warm morning sun humming to the song "Happy" by Pharrell Williams. She was happy because she'd just read an online review in the Napa Register News about her spa. *Ashley's Day Spa in Napa Valley is a hidden jewel that provides its customers with a tranquil and healing environment to rest and rejuvenate.*

Her day spa was a jewel because she'd set high standards for her workers to create a peaceful and harmonious environment, and handle customers with an even-tempered attitude at all times.

She drove up the circular driveway to her spa and stepped out of her convertible Miata. She listened in horror as Christina, her female masseuse, and India, her top hair stylist argued so loudly, that she could hear them from her car.

Ashley entered through the elegant glass doors and stopped at the receptionist's desk. The arguing immediately stopped. She looked around and exhaled when she saw there were no customers.

"What's the matter, Chris?" Ashley asked her best friend in a calm voice.

"India is cursing at me." Christina held her hands on her hips.

Ashley placed her briefcase and handbag on the receptionist's desk. She looked down and saw the edge of an envelope. She pulled it out and saw that it was her insurance bill stamped PAST DUE in large red letters. How did the bill get under the receptionist's counter? She shook her head and remembered that Christina had been handling the mail while Amara was on vacation. Ashley was too busy to deal with mail issues right now; she had to put out this fire between Christina and India. She walked over to Christina and took her by the hand and led her to the massage chairs in the manicure room.

"Come have a seat Chris. I want to talk to you."

Ashley and Christina met in middle school when both of their father's served in Desert Storm. During that time in their lives, they were both awkward teens with bad skin. When they turned sixteen, Ashley unlike Christina, had bloomed into an attractive woman of average height with a shapely figure and a creamy cinnamon complexion.

Christina grew into a plain woman with an uneven complexion and a stocky body.

"India come and sit with me. I want to talk to you." Ashley led India to the massage chairs in the manicure room. She sat between the two women.

"This is a place of healing. Our priority is to provide our customers with a peaceful and relaxing environment, so we cannot have any arguing."

"But Christina is always flirting with every man that walks through the door." India barked.

"This wouldn't have anything to do with the new barber I just hired, would it?"

"That's what this is all about," India said. "Christina is already dating the man."

Christina gave India a cool look. "You're just jealous because he didn't ask you out."

"Ashley's Spa has standards of conduct. I'd gone over that with both of you before you started working here. I'll remind you again that arguing in this establishment is off-limits. I'm calm right now, even though I just found my past due insurance bill under the receptionist's desk." She put emphasis on the words past due, while looking at Christina. "I expect the same attitude from you both. If you two must argue, wait until you are off work and away from these premises. Do you both understand me?"

Christina turned away, examining her nails. India nodded her head.

Ashley's voice had a soothing effect on them.

"Now, while both of you are at work, I expect you to

respect each other. No cursing or gossiping or loud voices. Why don't you both come into the break room and have a cup of chamomile tea with me? There are some positive things that want to share with you about each other."

The two women acted cordially toward each other in front of Ashley, but Christina cut her eyes at India, giving her an evil look, indicating that this fight was not over. Ashley put the entire incident behind her. She shared some of their positive attributes with them over a cup of tea. After the discussion, both women went back to their workstations, with a better attitude.

Ashley walked into her office and sat down at her desk. Leaning back in her chair, she opened up the bill. She immediately picked up her cell phone and called the insurance company. She hoped her insurance hadn't lapsed. If it had, she could always reinstate it by paying her bill with her credit card over the phone.

A man's voice answered the phone.

"I'd like to pay my bill over the phone with my

credit card." She gave the agent her name and credit card number.

"Okay Ms. Jacobs, let me pull your file."

Ashley gave him her account number.

"That policy lapsed on June first. You'll have to open up a new policy."

"Why can't I reinstate that policy?"

"Because your policy has passed its reinstatement date."

"Would you like to open a new policy?"

"Yes."

"I can help you or you can open a new policy online."

"Thank you. I'll open one online." Ashley opened her laptop, and logged on to the insurance website and opened a new policy. After she'd finished, she leaned back in her chair thinking about how the insurance lapse might affect her business. She couldn't recall any injuries or accidents in the spa during the time she was uninsured. She exhaled a deep breath, for all she knew all of her workers and customers appeared to be fine.

She thought about all of the changes she wanted to make to her spa. She wanted to add three more workstations, two more shampoo bowls, two hair dryers and another massage room in the back near the whirlpool.

Chapter 2

Justin Underwood navigated his forty-foot motor yacht under the Golden Gate Bridge in the salty morning air. Tall, dark and muscular, he was an attractive member of a line of handsome Underwood men who believed in protecting their loved ones. When it came to love, Justin was drawn to soft, desirable, intelligent women. One thing he couldn't stand was an argumentative woman.

Born into wealth and privilege, Justin was the family attorney and co-owner of Underwood Hills Winery in Napa Valley. He fought for the disenfranchised and equal rights for women. He'd won millions defending ordinary people in his private law practice located in downtown Napa.

Justin's grandmother had dubbed him the strong one, because he used his strength to stop fights among his brothers. On the surface, Justin appeared to be smooth, refined and faithful, surrendering himself to a higher authority. But underneath the surface, if pushed, he could become openly aggressive and domineering, calling himself "the boss" whose word was law.

"I still can't believe the jury awarded Ms. Lightfoot one and a half million dollars in her sexual harassment case," Hawk said.

Justin had given Hawk his nickname, because of his uncanny ability to find clues others overlooked when he investigated cases. Justin and Hawk had the same sturdy build and dark brown complexion, but Hawk didn't have Justin's good looks. Justin had one deep dimple in his left cheek. His dark brown eyes could be as hard as granite or as soft as a summer breeze.

Justin's jaw twitched at the thought of the burly prison guard and his supervisor lying under oath every time they took the stand. Fortunately, they hadn't fooled the jury or him. Justin had heard people lie under oath for as long as he'd been an attorney. He could smell a liar and a fraud a mile away.

"Ms. Lightfoot deserved the award considering all of the lies she's had to endure during the trial. I'm tired of watching women get abused by the system."

"I never asked you this, but why do you feel so strong about women's rights?"

"Because I watched my father smother my mother's dream of becoming a lawyer when I was growing up. He called that men's work and told her a woman's place was at home with her children. Then my mother left. She hasn't been back since."

"So that's why you're so passionate about equal rights."

"Yep. That's why."

"I'm glad I don't discriminate against babes. For all I care, my women can work wherever they want. All they need is a pretty face and a small waist." Hawk said.

Justin cringed at his friend's statement. "You sound like a chauvinist, Hawk."

"What?" Hawk hunched his shoulders.

"Women are not babes." Hawk's attitude was beginning to irritate Justin. He massaged his shoulder blade again. His stressful line of work caused him to suffer from muscle tension in his neck and shoulders.

Hawk observed Justin rubbing his shoulder. "You okay? You keep rubbing your shoulder."

"I need a massage, but my masseuse is on vacation."

"I read a review about a day spa this morning. It's supposed to be a great place to get a massage, relax and rejuvenate. Maybe you should call for an appointment."

"What's the name?"

"Ashley's Day Spa."

The next morning, Justin sat by his pool stretched out on his chaise lounge, rubbing his shoulder. He pulled his cell phone from his shirt pocket and googled Ashley's Day Spa.

Alonzo, his butler and chauffeur, brought out a tray with an iced coffee, croissant and fruit for Justin. Alonzo saw that Justin was on his cell phone, so he placed the tray on the buffet under the patio awning.

Justin saw Alonzo from the corner of his eye. "That iced coffee is calling my name, Zo."

Alonzo brought the iced-coffee over to Justin.

Justin was sipping his coffee when he heard a voice come on the phone. "I'd like to make an appointment for a massage today if possible."

"We don't take same day appointments for massages," the voice on the other end of the phone said.

"When can I get an appointment?" he asked.

"Two weeks."

"Two weeks! I can't wait that long. Do you have a manager?"

"One moment please."

"This is Ashley Jacob's. May I help you?" she asked in her soft voice.

"I need an emergency massage. Can you get me

in today?"

Ashley had planned to run some errands this morning. The only time she had available was in the late afternoon. "Normally we don't do same day massages, but maybe I can pencil you in my schedule toward the end of the day. How does four o'clock sound?"

"Four o'clock sounds great."

"Sign me up."

"What's your name?"

"Underwood. Justin Underwood."

***

As Justin exited his Black Escalade and walked from the parking lot into Ashley's Day Spa in the heat of the day. He wiped away a drip of sweat making its way down his neck. He'd arrived thirty minutes early because he wanted relief from his shoulder pain, and the spa was close to his home.

Once inside, he stopped at the receptionist's desk and said "I have a four o'clock massage."

"Is this your first time here?" The woman asked with an Ethiopian accent while looking in the appointment book. "Mr. Underwood?"

Justin nodded his head.

She handed him a questionnaire on a clipboard. "Please sit and fill this out. After you finish, I'll take you in the back to the whirlpool."

Justin took a seat while looking around the spa admiring the aqua and white color scheme with royal blue accents. He saw six hair stylists lined up in a row wearing aqua uniforms.

Women were seated under hair dryers, leaning their heads back in shampoo bowls, and sitting in tall chairs getting pedicures and manicures. Justin thought that he was the only male in the spa until he saw a barber in the rear of the salon shaving a man's head. He would be glad when his masseuse returned from vacation. He finished his paperwork and handed it back to the receptionist. He had one question that he reserved for his masseuse.

The receptionist led him down a long dim hallway that opened up into a large area with a whirlpool in a private room with the door wide open.

"Please stand on the scale." The woman weighed him and then took his blood pressure. She took his clipboard into the massage room and laid it on a table. "Have a seat right here. Your masseuse will be right with you."

While sitting in the chair outside the massage room, he spotted an attractive young woman wearing an aqua t-shirt and leggings sitting at a desk down the hall. She must be my masseuse; he thought. He tried to make eye contact to ask his question, but she didn't look up. He walked over to the woman. As he approached her desk, he accidently bumped into the side, knocking over an open bottle of water onto her lap.

Quickly picking up a box of tissue from the woman's desk, Justin said, "Pardon me for my clumsiness." He continued to apologize while dabbing the water from her desk. He expected her to yell at him. "I'm sorry," he apologized again, sopping up the water with a wad of tissues. After cleaning up his mess and collecting himself, he looked into the woman's face and thought he'd never seen a more beautiful woman.

"It's okay," Ashley said. "It's only water."

The sound of her exceptionally soft voice caught Justin's attention. Not only was it soothing, but her attitude was comforting as well. Tension melted from Justin's face. He expected her to yell at him because of this clumsy, awkward accident. Her voice, he thought, made him feel completely at ease. Something about her intrigued him. He'd never felt this comfortable around a gorgeous woman before.

He scanned the sexy woman for flaws, but couldn't find one. Her smooth, clear skin glowed like warm cappuccino. She wore her hair in a thick dark brown ponytail past her shoulders. He could see through her shirt that she had full jutting breasts, a narrow waist, and curvy hips.

Justin loved a woman with nubile curves. His last girlfriend was gorgeous with a body to die for, but her constant arguing made him feel tense all the time. He felt the exact opposite now in the presence of this woman. He gave Ashley a quick flash of his handsome smile. "Allow me to have your clothing cleaned," Justin offered.

Ashley's long lashes swept up from her high cheekbones. She gave him a reassuring look. "It's okay." She returned his smile with a wide toothy smile. "Don't worry. I'd planned to wash this uniform today."

Attracted to her good looks, silky voice and easy going personality, Justin had to get to know her better. He'd forgotten all about the question he had about his paperwork. "I'm sorry, let me introduce myself." Holding out his hand, he said. "I'm Justin Underwood." He looked into her eyes to see if she recognized the name. She didn't.

Ashley shook his hand and felt the warmth of personal contact in his hands. "I'm Ashley Jacobs, and you are my four o'clock appointment."

Justin's eyes shined as he patted some beads of water from her wrists with a clean tissue. He noticed that her grip was strong and her fingers slim. Standing at her desk still making eye contact, Justin pulled a business card from his wallet, placing it in her hand. "Since you won't let me have your clothing dry cleaned, at least allow me take you out to dinner."

"I'm sorry." She looked at the card. "Mr. Underwood, I don't date my clients," Ashley said.

Her rejection didn't bother him. He continued talking to her until she was ready.

"Are you ready for your massage?"

"Yes. I am."

Ashley appeared to be slightly distracted after taking one look at Justin's questionnaire. "I see that your blood pressure is very high." She gave him a serious look. "What kind of diet do you consume on a daily basis?

"Why would you ask me that?"

"I'd like to know if your diet is causing your high blood pressure."

Feeling relaxed hearing Ashley's voice, Justin offered. "Maybe my stressful line of work has something to do with it. I'm hardly ever at home and admit I don't eat right." Justin snapped out of the direction of their conversation. He didn't come here to talk about his blood pressure. He came here for a massage. His new goal was to get Ashley's cell phone number.

"I think, for your health, you can lower your blood pressure by slowing down and relaxing more. Stress can cause many health problems. I have several massage therapy programs perfect for reducing stress."

Justin fantasized about getting a massage from Ashley. "Massage therapy programs? Tell me more."

"Well…we offer several programs. The first one is my High Tech Massage that lasts for one hour. It focuses on the upper body and releases specific tension in the neck, shoulder, back, and forearms."

"That sounds good. What else do you have?"

"We have our Healing Stone Massage; it lasts for seventy-five minutes. You melt into and absorb soothing heat from our river worn stones. We use warm & cool stones."

"I know I don't want that. What else?"

"We also have our Hawaiian Lomi Lomi massage that lasts for one hour. It is a full-body massage. We work gently yet deeply into your muscles with continuous flowing strokes, totally nurturing your body, enabling you to relax and feel the Hawaiian Aloha."

"Aloha massage," he murmured. She reminded him of a Hawaiian hula dancer. He looked into her sexy brown eyes and said. "That's the one I want."

As a trained physical therapist and masseuse, the Lomi Lomi massage happened to be Ashley's specialty, but she didn't tell Justin.

"Why don't you disrobe and sit in the whirlpool for about thirty minutes. You can dry off with some towels and robes in there. I'll meet you in the massage room."

Justin went into the whirlpool room, breathed in the fresh air from the open windows, disrobed and relaxed in the warm rushing water.

Thirty minutes later, Ashley knocked on the door. "Mr. Underwood, are you ready for your massage?"

Justin had fallen asleep in the warm water. He woke up after hearing Ashley's voice. "I'll be right out." He walked into the massage room with a towel wrapped around his waist and saw Ashley rubbing warm lotion on her hands. She had changed into another uniform and placed a white sheet on the massage table leaving the hole uncovered.

"Lie on the table and place your face in the hole."

Justin obeyed Ashley's command.

Ashley stood in front of him and stroked the back of his shoulders. Her fingers warmed at the touch of his skin. The balminess moved up the length of her arm. She began rubbing the palms of her hands down his back away from his spine. She worked her way up and down his arms to the tips of his fingers. Her strong fingers squeezed the muscles in his legs down to his feet. Then she started again at his shoulders.

All Justin could do was moan and groan. He felt the Hawaiian Aloha of her touch heal his muscles with continuous flowing strokes nurturing his body. The sound of her voice healed his soul. "My masseuse never made me feel this good. Maybe I should hire you."

"I'm flattered Mr. Underwood. But I have too much work running my spa." She looked at the clock and saw that an hour had passed. "I'm finished." She said softly. "Do you feel the Hawaiian Aloha?"

"The Hawaiian Aloha?" Justin smiled and turned around on his back to look into her eyes. "It was totally relaxing. No wonder your spa garnered such great reviews. I feel like a million bucks."

Ashley smiled. "That's what I like to hear."

"Can I make another appointment for tomorrow?"

Ashley gave him a smug look. "Are you sure you need another massage that soon?"

"Yes. I do. But if you can't fit me in for a massage tomorrow, maybe you can fit me in for dinner."

"Dinner? No. I already told you I don't date my clients, Mr. Underwood."

"Call me Justin."

"Justin, here is my business card. You can call me at the spa when you're ready for another massage, but not for tomorrow. I'm all booked up."

"Thanks." He took her card and looked it over. "I'm very persistent, Miss Jacobs. "If you don't have dinner with me, I will just have to come here every day and wait for a massage until you say yes."

"You wouldn't."

"I would." He gave her a devilish grin. He was an expert negotiator.

"I guess it won't hurt to make an exception in your case Justin." Ashley thought he was handsome and polite, why not have dinner with him.

"You like Low Country cuisine?" he asked.

"Never heard of it."

"There's a first time for everything. When do you get off work?"

"I usually leave at six."

I'll pick you up tomorrow at seven. Is that

okay?"

"Seven is fine. I'll be here."

Chapter 3

A long black Lincoln limousine drove around the circular driveway and stopped in front of Ashley's Day Spa. Seconds later; Justin exited the back seat looking like he'd just stepped out of Hollywood wearing a slim fitting dark suit and Italian sunglasses.

"Wow! Who's that?" Le said in a thick Vietnamese accent. "He look like a movie star." Everyone ran to the front and peeked through the windows.

"That's Ashley's new boyfriend," Christina said turning up her nose.

"I'll be right back, Zo," Justin said as he walked up to the spa. Before he reached the threshold, Ashley met him at the front door wearing an after five dinner dress.

Justin's eyes swept over her body approvingly. "You're gorgeous."

Ashley ignored the compliment. "Seriously…a limo?" She gave him a cynical look. "You don't have to impress me."

An easy smile played at the corners of Justin's mouth. "I'm not trying to impress you. My limousine is the most convenient way for me to get around in the city most of the time."

India and Le exchanged admiring glances as they watched Justin help Ashley into the back seat. With an adventurous toss of her head, Christina turned around and walked away.

Justin could have taken Ashley to other five-star restaurants in Napa, but he wanted to take her to Poppy Hill, his brother and sister-in-law's restaurant right next door to his family's winery. When they pulled up to the restaurant, Justin pointed out Underwood Hill's Winery. "That's my family's winery," Justin said.

Ashley raised her brows. "Your family owns a winery?"

"The best in the Valley."

When they arrived at Poppy Hill, Ashley inhaled the scent of seafood the minute she walked through the door.

Kenton and Briana, Justin's brother and sister-in-law, greeted them when they walked through the door.

Justin introduced Ashley. "Ashley, this is my brother Kenton and his wife, Briana."

"Nice meeting you," Kenton said as he extended his hand.

"Welcome to Poppy Hill," Briana said.

Ashley shook hands with both of them.

Briana gave Kenton a loving look. Kenton gave Justin a look of approval at his choice.

"We reserved our best table for you," Briana said.

Trevor, the manager, led them to a table outside and pulled out a chair for Ashley. Justin sat down and picked up the menu. "I recommend Briana's Shrimp Ketigree."

Ashley looked around and noticed that their table was near a large stone fountain in the middle of the patio. "What a wonderful place to enjoy a warm summer evening."

Justin looked her over seductively. "You look lovely Ashley."

"Thank you." Ashley had chosen to wear a royal blue after five-evening dress accessorized with diamond jewelry and silver sandals. Justin chose to wear no tie. He hated ties because he always had to wear them in court.

Ashley looked up at the twinkling silver stars shining in the black sky.

Justin wondered what Ashley was thinking as he watched her staring into the starry sky. She looked like she was in another world. He wished he could see what she saw, and feel what she felt. He admired her serene outlook. Unfortunately, he didn't have that gift. His life was anything but serene. He dealt with hard core facts on a daily basis. That was why he had tension in his shoulders.

"So tell me something about yourself. How long have you been working as a physical therapist?"

"I've been a physical therapist for about four years. I opened my day spa shortly after I graduated from college."

"What college did you attend?"

"Sacramento State. I attended on a full academic scholarship and earned a master's in physical therapy."

"Why physical therapy?"

"I enjoy providing people with good health and nutrition. Physical fitness is important to me."

Justin couldn't understand why a person could be so passionate about physical fitness. Then he figured she was just as passionate about her profession as much as he was about the law.

"What about you Justin. I saw on your business card that you are a civil rights attorney."

"Yes. I am."

"That line of work sounds stressful."

"I specialize in domestic abuse, equal pay and sexual harassment cases."

"Seems like your body of work consists of fighting for women's rights."

"I'm passionate about being a voice for the voiceless in court."

"Oh. You're like a knight in shining armor, fighting to protect people." Ashley was impressed with Justin.

"So what made you want to become a civil rights attorney?"

"L.A. Law."

"Huh?" Ashley gave him a confused look.

"It was a television show in the 80's."

"Ah."

"I was ten years old when I decided to become a lawyer. I told my father that I wanted to be a lawyer like the ones on LA Law. When my brothers had fights, which was all the time, I held play court."

"Play court?"

"Yes. I played the lawyer and the judge and decided who was right or wrong."

"I'm surprised your father didn't want you to go into the family wine business."

"My father knew I didn't want to work in the wine industry. He watched me play court with my brothers and told me that my gift was the law. He said we needed a good lawyer in the family."

"He sounds like a great father."

He was a great father, but a terrible husband, Justin thought. "Fortunately my brother, Kenton loved working in the winery and the vineyard, so dad prepared him to take over the winery."

"Where did you go to law school?"

"Hastings, in San Francisco. After I graduated, I clerked with the mayor's private law practice and gained valuable experience working on civil rights and criminal cases. While I worked there, I gravitated to cases involving women's rights."

Justin had barely grown beyond his teenage years when his father passed away. His younger siblings, Carter, Brandon, and Crystal had long given up playing court. His oldest brother, Kenton had never played that game with them.

A decade later, Justin represented Kenton and the winery in several lawsuits involving bottlers. He helped his younger brother, Carter patent an invention that made him a billionaire. When his baby brother Brandon, got caught smoking pot with the wrong crowd, Justin kept him out of jail.

The waiter brought out their meals. "Mmmm… this shrimp smells good." Ashley said.

"I thought you'd like it." In between bites, Justin decided to ask Ashley a personal question. "So do you have a boyfriend?"

"Boyfriend? No. I broke up with him several years ago. He liked to argue, fuss and fight too much."

"But all couples argue."

"Not me. I won't allow anyone or anything destroy my peace of mind."

Justin gave her a surprised look. "That explains why you have such a soothing effect on me. I love your temperament Ashley." Something in Ashley's manner tamed the wild beast that roared inside Justin's body.

"Thank you."

Justin stared at this remarkable woman. He figured that she protected her peace of mind and environment, because she was a dreamer. He imagined her as a woman who saw the world through rose-colored glasses. He hoped her temperament wasn't a bad thing.

"You're staring."

"I'm sorry. I still can't believe that I spilled water all over you."

"You were worried about drying me off and cleaning my uniform." Looking into his eyes, she said, "You were so polite to clean up that mess."

"Believe it or not, I would have done anything to get close to you. I couldn't resist your reaction to my clumsy accident. I expected you to throw something at me or curse me out, but you did the opposite. Your kind words made me feel comfortable. And after hearing your sweet voice, I wanted to be in your presence. It's hard to find people like you in the world today, Ashley."

Smiling at Justin's compliment, Ashley said, "I'm glad you came in for a massage."

"Tell me about your family, Ashley."

"Not much to tell. I grew up in the Claremont area of Oakland. I have one younger sister and had an older brothers, but he died when he was in high school. We all had a good relationship with each other when we were growing up."

Justin listened as Ashley talked about her siblings, but he was quick to catch on to who she wasn't talking about—her parents. He'd been trained to listen to what people didn't say. He didn't want to bring up her parents because he knew she didn't want to talk about them, so he let it go. In the back of his mind, he made a mental note to find out more about Ashley's parents.

Later, that night, Ashley lay in bed, thinking about her date with Justin. She avoided committed relationships like the plague. She'd never had a serious boyfriend. She developed superficial intimate relationships, but she never allowed herself to get too close. She thought Justin was a good person, but wondered if she would eventually push him away like all the rest. She didn't understand why she did it, but it always turned out the same. She turned over in her bed and pulled the covers over her head. It was just a matter of time, she thought.

Chapter 4

Justin woke up with a sharp pain shooting down his neck. He popped two aspirins into his mouth and called Ashley to cancel his appointment for his scheduled massage. He had some work to do on his equal pay case. But, Ashley wouldn't let him get out of his appointment. She told him he could come after work because he was suffering from classic signs of stress.

It was mid-afternoon and the sun was high in the sky when Justin arrived at the spa. After walking through the sliding glass doors, he once again greeted Amara, the receptionist. "I'm here for Ashley."

Amara pushed a button on the telephone and said. "Please have a seat in the waiting room. She'll be out in a minute."

Justin walked past Christina on the way to the waiting room. Christina gave him a wink and a smile. She looked him over as if she were photographing him undressed with her eyes. She's flirting with me, Justin thought.

Justin sat on one of the four white leather chairs surrounding a circular coffee table. Crossing his legs on a white shag rug, he looked up and saw a large aqua wall that displayed Ashley's Day Spa in large stainless steel letters. He listened to the lulling sound of a waterfall flowing through speakers and closed his eyes.

Five minutes later, Ashley stood above him calling his name. "Justin," she spoke in her soft voice.

Justin's mouth turned up into a smile, and he opened his eyes. "Hey."

"Ready for your massage?"

"Sure."

"Follow me."

Justin followed Ashley down the hall into the dimly lit whirlpool room. "He loved that whirlpool.

"You know what to do," Ashley said before walking away.

Justin looked to his left and saw a white leather chaise lounge cattycorner to the whirlpool bubbling with lightly scented water. He couldn't detect the scent, but he thought it smelled like almonds. Ashley had filled it with warm water and bath salts while Justin was in the waiting room. A thick white terry cloth robe hung on a wood hanger from a free standing rack situated in a corner. Justin disrobed and sank into the bubbling water. He immediately fell asleep.

Fifteen minutes later when Ashley returned, Justin noticed she was barefooted, wearing a white leotard. He had dried off with a towel and slipped into a robe. Ashley led him into the massage room. She draped a large white sheet over the table leaving the hole open.

"Lie on the table and place your face in the hole." Seconds later she rubbed some warm oil onto her hands. "Is your shoulder still bothering you?"

"Just a little, but not as bad as before."

"You know, your stressful lifestyle is not conducive to good health. One remedy for your condition is to reduce the stress in your life."

"Any idea on how I can do that?"

"I recommend yoga and breathing exercises."

"Maybe I'll try that."

"To rule out a more serious condition," she asked. "Do you have pain in your chest area?"

"No."

"Good. Then let's start your Aloha massage." Ashley used the tips of her fingers and her palms to apply pressure to his shoulders and neck.

"Em, that feels so good."

Moving down the side of the table, Ashley stretched Justin's skin away from his spine until he groaned. With each touch of her fingers, warmth radiated throughout his body. He wanted to pull her into his embrace and make love to her right there, but he couldn't do that. He barely knew her. All he knew about her was what she told him at the dinner at Poppy Hill. Thinking back to their conversation, he wondered why she'd excluded her parents from her conversation. His thoughts prompted him to want to protect Ashley from any harm. Letting his arms go limp at the sides of the table, he said, "you are amazing." With each touch, he felt more comfortable with Ashley.

After the massage, Justin felt completely relaxed, better than he felt in a long time. "I have a question for you Ashley."

"What's that?"

"I would love for you to come to dinner at my house tonight."

"I don't think so."

"Oh come on. Don't give me that I don't date my clients excuse."

Ashley smiled. "I guess since I've already broken my rule, I may as well join you."

"Of course you should. We all have to eat."

It was after six when Justin and Ashley pulled up to Justin's estate. Ashley had no idea that Justin lived in such a lavish residence. Although she grew up in a middle-class family, Ashley felt comfortable around anyone. She had no interest in Justin's wealth.

Alonzo drove through the gate and stopped at the front door. Justin looked at Zo through the rear mirror and winked his eye, which meant Zo needn't open the door. Justin got out of the car and opened Ashley's door.

"Nice house." Ashley said.

"Thanks." Justin opened the front door.

Ashley walked over the threshold and stood in the marble foyer. A double staircase with iron railings curved its way upstairs. Looking ahead, she saw an elegantly furnished formal living room decorated in soft tones of grey and blue. In the distance, she saw an Olympic size swimming pool through the windows. Looking to her left, she saw a pale blue formal dining room with a large crystal chandelier hanging over the large table. On her right, she saw a dark wood paneled library with a big screen television and brown leather furnishings. Justin took her by the hand and led her into the living room.

"Before we have dinner, would you like a tour?"

Ashley nodded her head.

"Come on." Justin said as he grabbed her hand and walked with her throughout the house.

"I had no idea you lived like this Justin." She said looking him over.

"You don't hold it against me. Do you?"

"No. I didn't mean it like that. It's just so…so…big."

"Yeah, I have to agree. It's too much house for me. But it wouldn't be too large if I had a family."

Ashley looked at him sideways. "Are you planning to get married?"

"Eventually."

"Do you have anyone in mind?"

Justin smiled. "Maybe." He didn't want to scare Ashley off.

"My little townhouse is nothing like this."

"When are you going to invite me over?"

"You're welcome to my humble abode anytime." Ashley said.

"What's that wonderful smell?"

"Dinner. Let's go see what the cook has prepared." Justin led her into the dining room where Alonzo was arranging the meal on the table.

"I remember you said that you loved seafood. I had my chef prepare some salmon. I hope you like it?"

"I'm sure I will," Ashley said looking at the scrumptious feast set before her.

"Have a seat." Justin said, pulling out her chair.

After dinner, they went into the library for a drink. Ashley sat on the leather sofa.

"What would you like?"

"How about a glass of white wine."

Justin poured himself a brandy and poured some Chardonnay for Ashley. He brought both drinks over to the sofa that overlooked hills covered with vineyards. He handed Ashley her drink.

"So Ashley, tell me more about why you opened your spa?"

Ashley crossed her legs and took a sip of her wine. "After I'd graduated from college, I decided to start my own business rather than work for someone else. My best friend Christina was a physical therapy student too, but she dropped out several years before I graduated. She went back to college and worked with me at the spa until she graduated.

"You said Christina is your best friend?" Justin remembered Christina brazenly flirting with him at the spa. He gave Ashley a critical look. Was Ashley in denial about Christina's loyalty? No, he thought. He gave Ashley the benefit of the doubt and figured she didn't know much about Christina's character. He didn't want to get in the middle of their drama, so he kept his thoughts to himself and said nothing.

"Yeah, I've known Christina since middle school."

Justin took a sip of his brandy and listened tentatively, encouraging Ashley to continue.

"We grew up together. In middle school, we were together all the time, like bacon and eggs. I remember in the seventh grade Christina took up for me when this girl wanted to fight me because of my long hair. Christina is a little bigger, so she stood in front of me and told the girl "You have to go through me first." Christina made the girl back off. The girl left me alone. Since then, I've been a devoted friend to Christina.

"How is she working out in your spa?"

Ashley looked down and mumbled. She didn't want to talk about how Christina and India had been fighting over the new barber. She tried to change the subject by talking about the beautiful furnishings in Justin's house.

Justin was quick to catch onto Ashley's attempt to change the subject. He rephrased his question. "Is Christina working out well in your spa?"

Ashley broke down and admitted. "There's been a bit of friction between Christina and India lately. India is the spa's top hairstylist. It started after I hired Bradford, our new barber."

"Humph. Nothing worse than two women fighting over a man," Justin huffed.

"Yeah, I know." Ashley added. "Customer service is important to me. I work hard to provide a peaceful environment for my customers to relax. But when Christina and India start fighting, creating a ruckus, I feel like all of my hard work is going down the drain. I don't want my customers to start complaining."

"You don't deserve that. Why don't you fire them?"

"I can't fire them because they're both very good at what they do. Besides, I can't fire my best friend."

Ashley didn't want to bore Justin with her problems. She asked herself; why she was fooling around with Justin. She didn't have time to date Justin or anyone else for that matter. Looking at him gazing out the window, she answered her question. She enjoyed being in Justin's company. Maybe it was because of his sexy masculinity.

Justin put his brandy glass on a table and moved closer to Ashley, wrapping his arm around her shoulders. He looked her over seductively. "I haven't been able to stop thinking about you since I first met you."

Ashley was spellbound by the heart-rending tenderness of this handsome man.

His eyes dropped from her sexy eyes to her shoulders to her breasts. As his embrace tightened, his attitude became more serious. Ashley put her arms around his neck, and in one swift motion, she was laying in his lap. She settled back, enjoying the feel of his arms around her. She wound her arms inside his jacket and around his back prompting him to remove his jacket. His mouth covered hers hungrily sending spirals of ecstasy through her. His lips pressed against hers leaving her mouth burning with fire. Shivers of delight followed his touch as he roused her passion. Blood pounded in her brain, leapt from her heart, and made her knees tremble. She looked up at him, "we better stop while we're ahead."

"Oh baby, I want you so badly right now."

"No," Ashley said feeling she was getting too close. "I need to go. I didn't want to stay long."

Justin released her from his embrace. "Okay, I'll take you home."

When Justin returned from taking Ashley home,

he walked through his door and sat in his library staring through the window thinking about Ashley. Why did she push him away? Women didn't do that to him. It made him want her more. Maybe she needed distance, he thought. He decided to give her some space. His impression of Ashley was that she appeared to be at ease with herself and had a relaxed attitude about life. She came off as innocent, sweet and unpretentious. But Justin thought Ashley might have a blind spot when it came to Christina's loyalty.

Chapter 5

Briana woke up early in the morning feeling nauseated but decided to go to work instead of sitting around the ranch feeling sorry for herself. When she arrived at Poppy Hill, she greeted Trevor, her manager and told him she would be in her office if he needed anything. She immediately called Kenton on her cell phone. "Hi, Honey."

"Hey Baby, what's up?" Kenton greeted as he inspected some leaves in his vineyard.

"I'm going to call Granny and tell her about Justin and his date the other night." She said leaning back in her office chair.

Kenton stopped in his tracks. "I wouldn't do that; Honey." He knew how strongly Justin felt about his privacy. Justin rarely opened up to Kenton. When Justin did open up, it made Kenton feel closer.

"But, I've never seen him with a woman before. Why don't we both go over to Granny's and tell her together?"

"No, Briana."

"Why not?" She said rubbing her stomach.

"You should give Justin his privacy. What if

he's not serious about Ashley?"

"He looked serious," Briana said dryly.

"All Granny is going to do is call Justin and give him the third degree. Give him some space, Baby," Kenton advised.

"Alright, alright. I heard you the first time. He needs his privacy. Although I think you're wrong."

"Do what you want to do, Briana. But don't come running to me when Justin calls to chew you out."

"Chew me out? He wouldn't do that. At least I hope he wouldn't."

"I'm just warning you."

"Okay. Bye."

"Have a good day, Honey. Don't work too hard. Love you."

"Love you too."

Briana had no evidence that Ashley was Justin's new girlfriend, for all she knew Ashley could have been a client. But he would have introduced Ashley as one of his clients, but he didn't, so Briana acted on her instinct. She saw the body language, and the way Justin looked at Ashley. She knew in her gut that Justin was crazy about Ashley. She also knew how much Henrietta wanted to get all of her grandchildren married off to loving spouses. This information would be important for that reason alone, so she decided to take the chance and let the cat out of the bag. She dialed Henrietta's number on her cell phone. "Hi, Granny."

Henrietta was sitting in her purple reclining chair in her bedroom reading the bible when she picked up her phone. She had her land line telephone, snack tray, TV, bed and recliner all within reaching distance so she wouldn't have to stand up for anything. "How are you feeling?" Henrietta asked.

"I'm fine. The baby's fine. I called because I have something to tell you about Justin."

"Justin?" Henrietta perked up. "What is that?" She folded up her newspaper and tucked it inside her magazine rack.

"He brought a woman to Poppy Hill for dinner the other night."

"Oh?" Henrietta waited to hear more.

"They took a long time to finish their meal. Then they took a long walk around the restaurant and left."

"Who is this girl? Who are her people?"

"Her name is Ashley, and she owns a spa in Napa."

"Hmm. What else?"

"That's all I know."

"I can't wait to call Justin to ask him about this girl." Henrietta looked through her tattered personal telephone directory with scratched out phone numbers for all of her grandchildren. She searched for Justin's telephone number while she talked to Briana.

Briana's eyes widened. "Granny, you have to promise me not to call Justin and pry into his business. Let him call you," Briana advised. "I only told you because I wanted you to know that he's dating someone." Briana had a funny feeling right after she told Henrietta the news that she should have listened to Kenton's warning. She could feel in her heart that Granny was going to call Justin. She hoped Justin wouldn't be upset.

Henrietta rushed Briana off the phone. "I'll talk to you later Briana." Henrietta hung up and dialed Justin's cell phone. "This boy hardly ever calls me," she mumbled to herself.

In Henrietta's opinion, Justin was a loner who didn't need to be around other people. He was special to her because he was the grandson who listened in church, and surrendered himself to a higher authority. He was her generous, practical grandson with a can-do attitude. The one who took the initiative, and made things happen legally for the family business.

The Law Office of Justin A. Underwood, located on the third floor of a three-story stone building with white trim on a tree lined walkway near Main Street overlooking the Napa River. Every morning on the way to work, he passed the police and fire stations, the post office, the corner florist, Andy's Café, and an art gallery where Brandon sold his paintings. What he loved the most about his ride to work every day was passing the famous Napa murals on the corner of Main and First Streets.

Leaning back in his leather executive chair, Justin glanced up at his degrees and awards hanging on the wall. He along with three associate lawyers specializing in civil rights violations ran a tight law office, winning most of their cases. After taking a sip of his iced-coffee, he turned on his laptop and thought about dinner with Ashley at his house. His cell phone rang, breaking his thoughts.

"Justin." Henrietta said in her raspy voice.

"Granny?" He paused.

He knew Kenton or Briana had told her about Ashley, but he didn't think his grandmother would call this fast. He didn't have anything to hide, he thought. He knew when he met Ashley that she was the woman for him. She was more than just a pretty face. There was something ethereal about her. Maybe it was her voice, her attitude or her serene outlook on life, whatever it was; he wanted her to meet his family. "How are you?"

"I'm fine son. I haven't seen you in a long time."

"I know Granny. I've been busy lately." He opened a file to work on an equal pay case.

"Briana told me that you had dinner with a woman at Poppy Hill. I'm calling to invite you and your friend to Sunday dinner."

"What Sunday?" He ran his fingers down his silver tie.

"This Sunday."

"Who is she? Where is she from?" Henrietta asked sitting forward in her chair.

"Tell you what Granny. I'll ask her over for Sunday dinner, if she comes you can ask her those questions yourself." He said running his finger down a bronze sculpture of Blind Lady Justice sitting on his desk.

Justin loved his grandmother with all of his heart. When he was a boy, he found the best way to get her affection was to be her strong right hand when dealing with his brothers.

When Justin finished his conversation with his grandmother, he called Ashley. "Hey there."

"Hey, yourself."

"I have a quick question. Got any plans for

Sunday dinner."

"No."

"Have dinner with me at my grandmother's."

Ashley paused for a moment. She wondered what she would say to his family if they asked questions about her family. "Justin, I'm not sure if I'm ready to meet your family."

"My grandmother will love you Ashley." He wanted to tell Ashley how he felt about her, but he knew she wasn't ready.

"That's nice to know Justin, but I'm just not sure."

Ashley believed all romantic relationships would eventually end in pain and failure. She wasn't even aware of her problem.

"You're not getting serious are you?" She asked.

"No." Justin lied. "It's only dinner, nothing more. I promise I will not get serious."

"Okay, but remember, you promised."

Justin grinned. "I'll pick you up at three."

Chapter 6

Briana and Kenton greeted Justin and Ashley when they arrived at the Underwood estate. Briana was anxious to find out more about Ashley because she'd never seen Justin with a woman. Kenton had told her that he could count the women on one hand that Justin had brought home for the family to meet since they were in high school. When Justin and Ashley walked through the door, Briana got a closer look at Ashley and thought she was pretty.

Justin introduced Ashley. "Ashley you remember my oldest brother Kenton and his wife, Briana from the restaurant the other night."

Kenton held out his hand, "Nice seeing you again, Ashley."

Briana smiled at Ashley and shook her hand.

They all walked into the dining room and met Henrietta, sitting at the dinner table in her wheelchair. She held out her arms. "Justin. I haven't seen you for so long. Let me look at you."

Justin walked up to Henrietta, "Hi, Granny." He paused. "This is Ashley."

Ashley smiled and took Henrietta's hand. Henrietta pulled Ashley toward her, kissing her on the cheek.

Henrietta had an immediate liking to Ashley.

"Have a seat next to me," Henrietta said to Ashley.

Justin pulled out Ashley's chair, and then sat next to her. Kenton and Briana sat across from them.

Everyone was smiling and talking when Justin's siblings; Carter, Brandon, and Crystal walked into the dining room and kissed Henrietta on the cheek before taking their seats. Justin sat next to Carter. Brandon and Crystal filled the empty seats.

Once everyone had quieted down from the introductions, Kenton prayed over the dinner. After gazing at his grandmother confined to a wheelchair, Justin started off grace praying for his grandmother's health.

He was thankful for his grandmother who spent her life raising and guiding him and his siblings after their parents divorced. He remembered the day, she'd dubbed each one with a nickname to describe their character. Justin was "the strong one" because he carried the family with his strength in court. Kenton was "the protective one" because he protected the family and the business from rival competitors. Carter was "the gifted one," because he had the gift of genius. Brandon was "the artistic one" because he had a brilliant artistic eye. Crystal was "the tender one" because she loved animals.

Now they were all adults, but Henrietta still stayed involved in their lives. Her goal now was to make sure that each grandchild found a loving spouse to marry. Two years ago, she'd played matchmaker with Kenton and Briana before they married in Briana's poppy field. She'd seen each grandchild, with the exception of Justin, bring home dates for her to meet. Out of all of them, Justin was the one who savored his privacy.

After grace, Briana went into the kitchen to bring out dinner.

"Do you need any help?" Ashley offered.

Briana turned around. "No. But, thank you. Kenton, why don't you open a bottle of wine while I bring out dinner?" Normally, Henrietta's cook and longtime friend, Ruby Pitts, prepared and served family meals, but tonight, Briana prepared a Low Country meal for the family.

"Justin, where did you and Ashley meet?" Kenton asked as he filled everyone's glass—except Briana's.

"Ashley owns a spa in Silverado Hills." Justin replied.

Henrietta raised her eyebrows. "That's an exclusive area." She looked at Ashley. "How long have you owned your spa?"

"About four years."

Justin interrupted. "Ashley is a physical therapist. You must have her Aloha massage." He patted his right shoulder. "It took away the pain I'd been feeling in my shoulder."

"I have to remember that in case I need a massage," Kenton said.

"Where did you go to school?" Henrietta asked.

"I graduated from—"

Justin interrupted. "You guys are not going to interrogate Ashley tonight. She's here to meet you all, not recite her resume."

Henrietta changed her line of discussion. "I hear you had dinner at Poppy Hill?"

"Yes. The food was delicious." Ashley said. "This is my first time tasting Low Country cuisine."

"Briana can give you some of her recipe tips after dinner," Henrietta said.

Briana brought out a platter of Blackened Redfish surrounded with fried okra.

"We were just talking about your cooking, Briana." Henrietta said.

"I hope you like seafood." Briana said turning to Ashley. She knew Justin loved seafood because she'd served it to him on several occasions.

"Here, let me help you with that," Kenton said, taking the platter from Briana. He sat it in the middle of the table and then went into the kitchen to bring out more dishes. Briana took her seat and began passing around trays and bowls of scrumptious delights.

After dinner, Briana invited Ashley into the kitchen. "I love cooking Low Country cuisine," Briana said as they entered the kitchen.

"Dinner was delicious. Why is it called Low Country?" Ashley asked.

"Because it's from the coastal areas of South Carolina and Georgia. "What are some of your favorite recipes?" Briana asked as she placed left over food into plastic containers.

"I love my mom's coconut shrimp over white."

"Coconut shrimp. That sounds interesting."

"It's a Filipino dish. My mother's Filipino."

"Ah." Briana murmured.

"So where did you learn how to cook Low Country cuisine?"

"I graduated from Le Cordon Bleu."

"No wonder you're such a good cook."

"Your spa sounds wonderful Ashley. I'd like to

come there and get a massage or a makeover one day."

"You're welcome to come any time."

"You said your mom was from the Philippines; tell me more about your family."

Briana watched Ashley cross her arms and tense up.

Words wouldn't come out of Ashley's mouth. "Um…excuse me. I'll go clear off the table," Ashley said, quickly walking out of the kitchen.

Briana knew why Ashley didn't answer the question about her family. Earlier in the week, she had called Ray, the police chief and asked him to do a background check on Ashley's family. Briana had met some girls in high school and college who preyed on successful athletes and other wealthy men for money and status. Love was not in the equation for these women. Briana wanted to make sure Ashley was not one of those women.

Kenton walked into the kitchen carrying an empty bowl and platter, nearly bumping into Ashley walking out in a hurry.

Briana knew that Ashley was hiding a secret, so she decided to tell Kenton about Ray's background check. "Honey. I have something to tell you," she said taking dishes to the sink.

"What's that, Baby?" Kenton said following her to the sink with more soiled dishes.

"I asked Ray at the police station to run a background check on Ashley's family. Ray told me that, the police department had been called out to the Jacobs residence many times to break up family fights.

They both had their backs to the door as they stood over the sink rinsing out dishes for Ruby who had the night off.

Ashley walked back into the kitchen to tell Briana that she was leaving when she overheard Briana and Kenton talking about the police coming to break up her family's fights. Her hand flew to her mouth. Sheer dread crossed Ashley's face as she listened to them discuss her deep-seated secret about her family. She rushed out of the kitchen without Briana and Kenton realizing that she'd overheard them.

Ashley returned to the dining room and stood over Justin, whispering in his ear. "Do you think we can leave right now?" She paused to think of a reason for leaving in a hurry. "I have a big day tomorrow."

Justin looked up into her face. "Sure, Ashley. We can leave now." He wondered why she was in such a hurry. Then the thought occurred to him that his nosey family may have said something out of line, rubbing Ashley the wrong way. He frowned at the thought. That's why he was so private about his personal life and never brought women around. He stood up and said his farewells to Henrietta, Brandon, Carter and Crystal. They all stood up and said goodbye to Ashley.

"Come back and see me again Ashley," Henrietta said.

"I will Mrs. Underwood. It was nice meeting you all." Ashley said in a calm voice.

Briana came out of the kitchen and gave Ashley a probing look. She was still waiting for an answer to her question, but she let it go since they were leaving. "It was nice meeting you Ashley. I look forward to seeing you again." Briana said.

Ashley lowered her eyes and walked away.

Justin knew something was wrong with Ashley. On the ride home he said, "Briana must have asked you some personal questions in the kitchen."

Ashley looked into his eyes. "How did you know?"

"Because I know my sister-in-law, and you came out of the kitchen ready to leave so fast."

"I'm sorry, Justin. I wasn't prepared to answer her questions about my family."

"I'm sorry, too. I know how nosey they can be.

I hoped they wouldn't pry." He moved closer to her placing his arm around her shoulders. "You know what you need?"

"No. What do I need?" Ashley said, rolling her head on his uninjured shoulder.

"You need to spend a day sailing with me on the bay tomorrow."

"Sailing on the bay?"

"Um hum. When I want to get away and relax, I take my boat out on the bay, throw on the music and kick back. Do you want to join me?"

"It sounds relaxing. I don't have any clients tomorrow. Yes. I'd love to join you."

***

Later that night, Ashley stood in front of her bedroom mirror thinking about dinner with Justin's family. They all seemed like nice people. Kind of nosey, but nice. Ashley felt ashamed of walking away from Briana when she'd asked about her family. She just clammed up. Words wouldn't come out of her mouth. Her mind shifted to Justin.

Justin had a way of taking her away from her problems. He was a wonderful man, and she knew he was getting serious about their relationship. She wanted to be honest because she couldn't bear hurting him. She searched her heart to find out why she'd been unable to totally commit herself in past relationships, but she came up with nothing.

She slowly slid the comb through her hair, falling into a daydream. In her mind, fog covered the mirror blocking her view. As the fog cleared, she smiled when she saw an image of Justin come into focus. He was standing behind her holding her in his embrace, on his yacht. They both had their hands on the steering wheel, guiding the yacht on the bay. Justin kissed her softly on her neck. He pointed out the Golden Gate Bridge in the distance. She smiled at him and then snapped out of her daydream back into reality. Her eyes softened. She wanted so badly to have a romantic relationship with Justin, but something was holding her back.

Chapter 7

It was five o'clock in the afternoon when Justin and Ashley walked onto the swaying pier at the Napa marina. They stopped at a berth where Justin docked his yacht; The Habeas Corpus.

"Here's my Baby," Justin said, kneeling down, stroking his yacht. He wore his usual sailing gear— chino shorts, classic polo shirt, deck shoes and Italian sunglasses. "I'm glad you're here," he said, scanning Ashley's shapely body clad in white pleated shorts, a navy blue t-shirt and white sneakers.

Justin took Ashley's hand to steady her. They climbed a stainless steel ladder to the second level and stepped into the forward cockpit. "I have a relaxing day planned us. All I want you to do is relax."

"Thanks." Ashley looked at him with amused wonder. "I had no idea you were a yachtsman."

"Yep. I'm a member of several yacht clubs around the bay. I rowed with the North Bay Rowing Club in Napa when I was in high school.

"Did your row team participate in any races?"

"We trained and raced in local competitions. I'm not big on racing anymore. I spend my time

pleasure cruising in the bay. Come on. Let's go."
He paused for a moment and asked, "Do you know
how to swim?"

"No, I don't."

He pulled an orange life jacket out of a deck box
and said, "Here, wear this. You're much too
precious to lose overboard."

Precious. What a nice thing to say, Ashley
thought. She took the life jacket and pulled it over
her head. Justin helped her fasten it in the front.
The mere touch of his hands sent a warm shiver
through her body.

Justin could feel what Ashley was feeling. He
pulled her hands, drawing her closer to him. Ashley
lifted her arms around his neck. In one forward
motion, she was in his embrace. He kissed her with
his eyes at first, then with his lips that were gentle.
His tongue sent shivers of desire racing through
Ashley's body. His lips seared a path down her
neck and shoulders, then reclaimed her mouth. She
returned his kiss with reckless abandon. The touch
of his lips on her sent a shock wave through her
entire body. "We... better... go now," Justin said.
Between each word, he planted kisses on her neck
and mouth. He left Ashley's mouth burning with
fire. She stood there with her eyes still closed.
Justin laughed, "Come on, Baby."

Ashley opened her eyes staring at Justin's
handsome face against the clear blue sky. "You're

a great kisser."

He gave her a seductive look. "I'm great at a lot of things."

Ashley tested the security of the strings on the life jacket and then followed Justin into the saloon. She watched him open the sunroof and the sliding doors in the cockpit area to air out the yacht.

"Are you ready for our voyage?"

Ashley had never been on a yacht. "Are you going to give me a tour before we get started?"

"Sure. Let's do that right now." Justin walked with Ashley on the main deck through the saloon with custom sofas covered in brown and tan leather. They walked into an alfresco dining area with a white banquette covered in navy and white striped cushions surrounding a dining table with navy blue director's chairs. They walked through the galley, outfitted with cherry cabinetry and black granite counters. After walking downstairs, she stuck her head inside the guest bath and cabin covered in teak wood paneling. Finally, they walked in the owner's stateroom furnished with a king bed covered with a navy Hermes cashmere blanket and a white leather headboard. She peeped into the lounge area and saw a white linen sofa, a wood cocktail table, and a desk with a white leather stool.

"So what do you think?" Justin asked.

"It's beautiful, Justin. Why do you call it The Habeas Corpus?"

"It's just a legal term."

"What does it mean?"

"It means that a detainee can seek relief from unlawful imprisonment." He took her hand and they walked back up the staircase to the cockpit. Justin sat in front of the large wood steering wheel and started the engine. He pointed to the seat next to him covered with a navy blue and white striped cushion. "Have a seat, Sweetness. You don't mind if I call you Sweetness?" Justin called her that because of all the women he'd ever met, she was genuinely nice. He also sensed that she needed him more than she'd ever admit.

"Sweetness. I like it." Ashley said admiring him steering the yacht. She looked out into the water and whispered, "Déjà vu."

"What?" Justin asked.

"Nothing. I'm just thinking about a daydream."

"Speaking of dreams, my dream is to sail the Habeas Corpus around the world."

Ashley imagined Justin doing just that. "That sounds romantic, sailing around the world."

Looking through the sliding glass windows,

Justin steered the yacht out of the marina. He sailed down the Napa River out to the San Pablo Bay.

Justin steered the yacht, keeping an eye on Ashley. Once he'd left the San Pablo Bay and entered into the San Francisco Bay, he saw a large group of sea lions swimming toward Fisherman's Wharf. "Look over there," Justin said, pointing to the sea lions.

Ashley walked over to the starboard side of the yacht, bent over the hull and stared at the huge mammals swimming and sunning on the pier. Her eyes widened in wonder.

Justin noted. "They're on the way to Fisherman's Wharf."

Ashley said. "Yeah, where they sit all day. I see them on the news all the time."

Justin enjoyed taking his yacht out on the bay. He'd already sailed down to Acapulco several times where he owned a condo. He had plans to sail down to Panama in the near future.

As they came closer to the Golden Gate Bridge, Ashley leaned against the port side of the yacht and felt a splash of salt water spray on her face. Turning around, she wiped the water from her face and thought how much she was enjoying the ride. She inhaled the fishy scent of the ocean and looked out into the vast Pacific Ocean beyond the bridge. Suddenly she saw a spout of water shoot up into the air.

"Justin?"

"What?"

"I think I just saw a whale."

Justin laughed. "You probably did. Blue whales are always around this area this time of year."

Before they reached the bridge, Justin steered into the Sausalito Marina. After docking, they both disembarked onto a long dock that led into the Sausalito Yacht Club. Ashley's legs felt wobbly as she walked up the dock. Justin grabbed her by the waist and took her inside a large reception area, and then into a restaurant where they were greeted by a hostess.

"Nice to see you again, Mr. Underwood."

"Good afternoon Kelly. We'd like to have lunch for two."

"I'll get a waiter for you right away."

A waiter led them through the dining room, filled with casually dressed people. They followed him to a table by a large window overlooking the bay. The dimly lit dining room felt casual and comfortable with its captain's chairs, wood paneling and nautical decorations. Soft music piped through the speakers. There was a bar in the center of the room. "Want a cocktail before lunch?"

"No. I'm not a big drinker."

When the waiter came to their table, Justin ordered sea scallops for them both. A soft smile crossed his face as he thought back to the day he spilled water all over Ashley. He was unaware that Cupid had creeped up on him and pierced his heart with an arrow. The next thing he knew, he was in love. The moment he heard Ashley's sultry voice and felt her gentle touch, he knew she was the right woman for him. He'd met many women in his line of work, but he'd never met a woman who soothed his soul and made him feel comfortable simply by being in her presence. His main requirement in a woman was that he had to feel comfortable around her. His feelings for Ashley grew stronger as the days passed. He wondered how she felt about him. He had to let her know how he felt. He took her hand and kissed it gently, his eyes clung to hers as he confessed. "You got me going, Baby."

Ashley's heavy lashes that shadowed her cheeks flew up. "I enjoy your company too Justin." Ashley felt deep affection for Justin. She liked how safe she felt in his strong arms. Steadying her gaze, she hoped she wouldn't revert to her non-committal, evasive ways, like she'd always done when she found herself in hot and heavy situations.

Justin exhaled at Ashley's revelation. One thing he refused to do was pursue a one-sided relationship.

After they had finished lunch, they boarded the Habeas Corpus and sailed back home in the sunset.

Justin walked Ashley to the door when they arrived at her home.

"You were right," Ashley said.

"Right about what?" Justin asked inquisitively.

Right about me needing a trip on the bay. "There's something about water that soothes my soul." She touched the side of his face with the palm of her hand. Her eyes were soft and gentle. "Thank you for taking me to Sausalito today. I was a little nervous meeting your family last night, but now, thanks to you, I feel back to normal."

"It was nothing."

"No. It was something," Ashley said, moving closer into his embrace. She buried her face in his neck and breathed a kiss there. Justin's lips traced the soft fullness of Ashley's lips and sent her flying in the pit of her stomach. She knew she'd better stop while she was ahead. After Justin had left, she turned around and quietly closed the door.

Chapter 8

Justin had convinced Ashley to introduce him to her parents. Ashley reluctantly agreed. Later on a warm August night, Justin picked up Ashley in his limousine. As the limousine drove up in front of her parents' three-bedroom, two bathroom, ranch style home, Justin looked through the window and saw someone peek through the living room curtains.

Ashley studied Justin to get his impression of her parent's modest home. She couldn't read his expression.

Justin could care less where Ashley lived. Wealth or the lack of it didn't mean anything to him when it came to Ashley. He only knew that he craved her kisses, her sultry voice, and the way she made him feel. Nothing else was important. Her parents couldn't be too bad to raise a woman as sweet as Ashley. But he wanted to know why she avoided talking about them. Anything he would learn about them tonight, whether good or bad, didn't matter.

An older Asian version of Ashley opened the door wearing a pale blue shirt dress and loafers. Ashley's mother gave Ashley a big hug. Ashley's pot-bellied African American father had an almond complexion and brown freckles. He hugged Ashley while looking at Justin, wearing a white open collar shirt and dark slacks. Justin walked in and held out his hand.. "Justin Underwood," Justin said leaning into the handshake.

Ashley's father shook Justin's hand. "David Jacobs, my wife's name is Cynthia."

Justin inhaled the sweet scent of coconut as he walked into the pale yellow living room with oak hardwood floors. There was a green and gold floral sofa and a matching loveseat in the middle of the living room. A large mirror with no frame hung on the wall above a red brick fireplace. A wood mantle supported a dark green vase filled with yellow roses, flanked by two white porcelain doves. Photos of Ashley's siblings hung on the living room wall with brass birds mounted in between.

"Come on in," Ashley's father said leading Justin to the sofa. "Have a seat."

Justin and Ashley sat down on the sofa. Ashley's parents sat in two gold velveteen reclining chairs bordering the fireplace.

"What happened to the coffee table?" Ashley asked in an uneasy voice.

Her parents gave each other hard looks. Ashley's mother changed the subject. "You two hungry? Dinner's ready." She stood up. "Let's go into the dining room."

Justin and Ashley followed her into the dining

room while Ashley's father remained seated giving his wife a mean look.

"Have a seat," Cynthia said. "I'll be right back."

Justin and Ashley took seats facing the window looking into the backyard. Justin's mouth watered at all of the appetizing dishes Mrs. Jacobs brought out and placed on the lazy Susan in the center of the table. Although it was dusk, Justin could see a large redwood tree taking up most of the space in the backyard. He inhaled the sweet scent of the coconut shrimp, and the heavy scent of garlic and curry coming from the other dishes.

"I felt like I couldn't go wrong with my coconut shrimp and green beans." Cynthia said. She'd spent all day yesterday preparing a large batch of Lumpia for appetizers.

"Everything smells delicious Mrs. Jacobs," Justin complemented.

Ashley's father entered the dining room wearing his Desert Storm veteran's cap. He took his seat at the head of the table while Ashley's mother sat on the opposite end.

"You know you're not supposed to wear your hat at the table," Ashley's mother criticized.

"I'll wear what I want at my own dinner table, Woman! Including my birthday suit if I want to!"

Justin stared straight ahead while Ashley lowered her head.

"Here we go," Ashley whispered under her breath.

Justin heard Ashley.

Ashley listened to them arguing over the cap for two minutes. "Mom! Dad! Stop it please," she said to stop the fight that she knew was coming.

"He knows he's not supposed to do that."

"Mom. Dad. Please don't do this in front of Justin. Ashley cracked a nervous smile. "Think of it this way mom, you won't have to look at dad's bald head."

"What was that you said?" Her father said, glaring at Ashley.

Ashley had a dazed look in her eyes. She remained quiet and turned her attention to Justin and her mother who were talking about the weather.

After dinner, Ashley and her mother brought out some vanilla ice cream in dessert glasses. Ashley's mother handed Justin his ice cream. Justin thought it was odd that Mr. Jacobs was holding his fork to eat his ice cream. Cynthia lay her arm on the table to hand her husband his ice cream when he suddenly lifted his fork ready to stab her in the arm.

Justin grabbed Ashley's father's arm in a strong grip. "I wouldn't do that if I were you, Mr. Jacobs." Justin said in a stern voice with no vestige of sympathy in its hardness. He pushed his chair back ready to protect Ashley and her mother.

Ashley jumped back. "Oh, no." she said, holding her hands up to cover her face.

"Get your hands off me. You can't tell me what to do in my own house." Her father said while swearing at Justin.

Justin turned his attention to Ashley's mother who'd run into the kitchen. She came out with a butcher knife, mostly for show. Justin calmly took the knife from her hand when she reached him. Ashley's parents argued like cats and dogs.

"Do I need to call the police?" Justin said to both of them.

They both quieted down.

Justin had to get Ashley away from this house. "Come on Ashley, we better leave." He pulled out his cell phone and called Alonzo. "We're ready, Zo."

***

They waited outside for about five minutes until Alonzo drove up. On the way home, Ashley was silent. When they got to her house, Justin walked her to the door. "Let's go inside and talk for a while."

Justin held Ashley's hand as they sat on the sofa. She yielded to compulsive sobs and then hot tears ran down her cheeks. Justin let her cry her heart out. It broke his heart to watch Ashley shed tears. He swept her hair away from her face and rubbed her back to comfort her. He would endure any hardship to take away her pain.

His feelings turned to anger as he thought of her parents. He asked himself why they would fight like that when they knew they were meeting him for the first time. Didn't they have enough sense to wait until they were alone before they started fighting, especially over something as trivial as a hat? He wondered if they argued like that all the time or if this was just a fluke argument. The fact that they fought like that at all made him understand why Ashley avoided talking about them. She was embarrassed by them. How could a woman as serene as Ashley come from such a violent family?

Justin was amazed to see how expertly Ashley used humor, about the hat and his bald head, to keep the peace between them. He watched her sooth her father's anger and her mother's criticism. When her peacekeeping attempt had failed, he watched Ashley withdraw into another world. As a trained attorney, Justin knew the importance of maintaining positive communication in toxic situations. He was embarrassed for Ashley, because of her parent's behavior. He asked himself a hard question. Did he want to marry into this violent family? He wondered if her parents would get along with his family. He had a million questions, but he didn't have the heart to ask Ashley for any answers right now. Instead, he let her cry.

"You all right?" Justin asked, rubbing her back.

"I'm okay now. Thank you."

"You don't have to thank me, Baby. Do you want to talk about what happened?"

"There's nothing to talk about."

A red flag raised in Justin's mind. Ashley must be immune to her parent's behavior if she thought there was nothing to say. "Nothing to talk about?" he asked.

She smiled. "Nothing," she said burying her feelings.

Justin wondered how her parent's behavior had affected Ashley.

"I don't react to conflict between my parents," she said reading Justin's mind. "I refuse to be anything like them or have a relationship anything like theirs."

Justin lay back on the sofa and listened to Ashley open up about how she rejected their fighting. Justin's mouth opened. That's why she reacted so calmly when he spilled the water on her at the spa, he thought. She had learned not to react to surprises.

"My father suffers from PTSD. When he came back from Desert Storm, no one knew what it was. My family just coped with his illness then and now. I have tried to get him to go to the VA for counseling for years, but he refuses. He thinks counseling is for the weak." Memories crossed Ashley's mind of her father chasing her down the street on her thirteenth birthday. All she could remember was her heart beating hard in her chest as she ran for her life. Her father had forbidden her from seeing a high school boy. One day her father saw the boy walking Ashley home from school and ran him off. After that, her father chased her down the street, cursing at her for disobeying him. Ashley ended up at Christina's house until her mother came and picked her up later that night.

Tears welled up in her eyes again as her mind drifted to thoughts of her oldest brother. He was the real reason she'd cried on Justin's shoulder. She'd given up on her parent's dysfunctional relationship years ago. But the pain of losing her brother always haunted her every time she visited her parent's home.

"Remember that night at Poppy Hill when I told you my oldest brother had died." A pain tightened in her throat. She swallowed hard.

Justin nodded his head while he held her hand.

"Yes, I remember."

"Well, I didn't tell you why my brother died," she said lowering her gaze.

Justin raised a brow, hoping she wasn't about to tell him something horrible. "You don't have to talk about this if you don't want Sweetness."

"No. I want you to know the truth about my family. When my brother, Derek, was a senior in high school, he brought his girlfriend over for dinner one night. Our parents started arguing in front of her, just like they did tonight. I tried to stop the arguing, but nothing seemed to work. After dinner, Derek drove his girlfriend home. On the way, she broke up with him. She told him she didn't think her family would accept my family." Ashley's eyes reflected the pain she felt deep in her soul. "The next day, I came home from school and found Derek hanging from the tree in our backyard."

Stunned and dazed, Justin saw raw hurt reflected in Ashley's dark eyes. He could imagine her brother's body hanging from that tree in her family's backyard.

"Derek was crazy about that girl." She lowered her head. "He hung himself because of my parents. I blamed myself for years because I wasn't able to stop them from fighting that night." She lay back on the sofa staring at the ceiling. "I failed."

Ashley continued to open up about her relationship with her family. "When I was growing up, I was the family peacemaker. Whenever my parents got into fights, I tried my best to break it up. When I couldn't stop them, I'd sit on the back porch and sing a happy song while I looked at the sky. I remember my mother coming on the back porch with a black eye criticizing me. She accused me of having my head stuck in the clouds. She accused me of sweeping my problems under a rug, rather than dealing with reality." Ashley gave Justin a painful look. "I hate those words. My head was not in the clouds. I do deal with reality. I just don't drown in negativity like she does. I'm an optimist. I choose to look at the positive side of things instead of the negative. But my mother always found words to make me feel inadequate."

Justin could see the pain in Ashley's eyes. After watching her parent's violent behavior, he understood why it was important for Ashley to maintain her peace of mind. It was her way of coping and dealing with her family's violence. He also understood why she withdrew. But when Ashley withdrew from conflict, he thought she must have harmed herself and others by not facing dishonest people and her problems.

Justin knew that Ashley's desire to maintain her peaceful persona was unrealistic because conflict was a natural part of life. Everyone had to face hostility at one time or another. Even though he loved Ashley's warm, sweet personality, he wanted her to put her fears aside and learn how to face discord and conflict. He'd watched her ignore Christina's true character. He decided right then and there that Ashley needed him more than she realized. He was determined to carry Ashley's weakness with his strength.

Chapter 9

Justin sat in his home office looking over a case file when his cell phone rang. He looked at the screen and saw that it was his grandmother.

"Hi, Granny."

"Hey, Baby. I called to tell you that I like your friend Ashley."

"Thanks, Granny. She loved Briana's cooking."

"I have to admit son, I'm happy to see you dating. I was beginning to wonder about you."

"Come on, Granny. You know I'm straight. I'm just a private person."

"Yes, I know you value your privacy, but don't get to be so private that you forget about those who love you."

"I've been busy with work Granny. What do you need?"

"I called to encourage you to continue dating Ashley. She seems like a sweet girl."

"She is sweet, Granny."

"Tell me about her."

Sighing heavily at his grandmother's prying, he knew if he didn't answer her question, she would keep snooping until she found out what she wanted to know. He decided to open up about Ashley. "Okay Granny, I'll be honest with you. I don't know a lot about Ashley. All I know is that I'm attracted to her warm personality, good looks and the sound of her voice."

"The sound of her voice?" Henrietta brought her hand to stifle her laugh. "Boy! You're so funny. Only you would be attracted to a woman because of her voice."

Justin chuckled. "Yeah Granny. Isn't that strange? I find her soothing voice irresistible." He paused. "I've never met a woman who makes me feel so comfortable. She's unlike any woman I've ever met. She has a natural sense of humor and an easy laugh that I love to hear. She's the perfect woman except for one thing."

"What's that son?"

"You know how I feel about domestic violence."

"Yes, I know."

"Her father is abusive to her mother. He has PTSD. I had to stop him from stabbing her mother in the arm with a fork the other day. Ashley is the peacekeeper in her family. She's stopped her parents from fighting since she was a kid."

"No."

"Yes, Granny."

"I love her enough to marry her, but I don't know about her father. I can't imagine what I'd do if he ever hurt Ashley."

"Honey, don't you worry about her father or his PTSD. They used to call that shell shock back in my day. Just remember, you're not marrying her father. If you do marry Ashley, you don't have to go around him that much. Maybe once or twice a year."

"But what about her mother? I can't separate Ashley from her mother."

"She and her mother can go out to lunch and shop together. Or you can tell that joker he better not lay his hands on Ashley or her mother in your presence. Tell him how you feel, son."

"I've already told him that, Granny. But I think I'm going to have another talk with him."

"Good."

"I just want to get Ashley away from him."

"As long as you are her protector, he won't hurt her. Men who will fight a woman will not fight another man."

"Thanks Granny for the talk. I feel better

talking to you. I just hope her father doesn't become an obstacle because I love Ashley, and I want to marry her."

A wide grin crossed Henrietta's face. She felt like jumping for joy, but she controlled her emotions. "He won't be an obstacle unless you let him. Be patient with Ashley and focus on loving her. And please don't be so private that you forget about your family. Remember I'm always here for you."

"Thanks, Granny."

Chapter 10

Justin stood on the fueling dock at the Napa Marina watching an attendant pump diesel fuel into The Habeas Corpus while he visualized making love to Ashley. He loved being in her presence, and never wanted her to leave his side. He'd recently purchased a ring and decided to ask Ashley to be his girlfriend. Looking up from his watch, he saw Zo drive up with Ashley.

He walked down the dock and met Ashley at the curb where Zo had parked the limousine. He opened Ashley's door. At first, he saw her long copper leg step out of the limousine, and then she looked up into his face with her sexy eyes. Smiling, she looked casual yet elegant wearing white shorts, a navy blue t-shirt and deck shoes. Justin wore his normal sailing gear. "I'm glad you're here," he said scanning her body up and down.

Alonzo stepped out of the limousine and took her luggage out of the trunk.

"Just take it on the yacht, Zo," Justin said. "Take that cooler over there on deck too." He'd filled a cooler with bottled water, wine, cheese and fruit.

Turning his attention back to Ashley, Justin lifted his elbow for her to insert her arm. Escorting her to the dock, he said, "I have a relaxing weekend planned us. I forbid you to think about your problems."

"You don't have to forbid me to think about my problems—that's the last thing I want to do."

There was something warm and enchanting about her laidback attitude that he loved. He knew they would enjoy the weekend trip. "Come on. Let's go sailing." As they boarded the vessel, he steadied her balance.

Before they reached the Golden Gate Bridge, Justin steered into the Sausalito Marina. After docking, they both disembarked onto a long dock that led into the Sausalito Yacht Club. Alonzo had driven to the yacht club and was waiting for them at the curb.

They both entered the limousine. When they arrived at his residence, Ashley looked through the limousine window and saw a large three-tiered redwood building with one condominium occupying each floor. "This is it. I'm on the ground floor." Justin stepped out and opened the limousine door for Ashley. After they had walked inside, Ashley looked around at the modern furnishings with black leather furniture and floor to ceiling windows in each room. Abstract artwork graced each of the walls. "Wow. Where did you get this great artwork?"

"Most of the pieces were painted by my brother,

Brandon."

"And the sculpture."

"Most of it is by local artists in Sausalito."

"Here let me give you a tour." He led her through the condominium. "This is the living room."

Ashley walked up to the twelve-foot floor to ceiling glass windows, overlooking a view of the San Francisco Bay. Justin opened the sliding glass door leading onto his deck that wrapped around the entire condominium.

"It's beautiful," Ashley said following Justin.

"I like to throw something on the grill when I come here and kick back."

"I watched 'The America's Cup' races right from this chair," he said pointing to a cushioned chair. "But I had to use binoculars."

"That must have been amazing. I didn't follow the race. Who won?"

"Oracle." He paused turning to look into the kitchen. "Getting hungry?"

"Yes, I am."

"When I come here, I have my housekeeper stock the refrigerator and pantry. Let's take a look and see what's in the fridge."

They walked into the kitchen. Ashley admired the dark cherry cabinets, granite counters, and stainless steel appliances. Justin opened up the refrigerator and saw it filled with salmon steaks, chicken breasts, beef steaks, fresh veggies, a couple of lobsters and dairy items. "Guess I'll throw these steaks on the grill."

"I don't eat red meat, remember?"

"That's right, you love seafood." He pulled out the salmon steaks and said. "We can have these instead."

"Better. Are those asparaguses in that bag?" Ashley asked.

"Yeah. We can add those on the menu too. Ever tasted grilled asparagus?"

"No. I haven't."

"Don't worry. You'll love the way I grill them."

"Sounds like a plan."

"Want to sit out on the deck and have a glass of white wine before we start cooking?"

"Okay."

Justin went inside and came back with a bottle

of white wine and placed it on the table with two glasses. I found this Riesling wine at a local winery. My brother tells me that our winery will start producing white wines in about three years.

He lit the grill and went back to the kitchen to season the salmon steaks. Minutes later, he brought them out and threw them on the grill. "When the sun goes down, it can get cool on this deck. Let me know if you get cold."

"Okay. But why don't you let me season the asparagus for grilling," she offered.

Justin nodded his head while he kept an eye on the grill. "It only needs salt and pepper."

After dinner, they sat on the deck, finished the bottle of wine, and watched the sunset. Ashley rubbed her arms and legs.

Justin could tell she was getting cold from the breeze off the bay. "I'll be right back." He went into his bedroom and put a Tiffany's ring box into his pocket. He came back with a black mink throw, a gift from his billionaire brother, Carter from his trip to Russia. "Here let me wrap this around you to keep you warm." He draped the fur around the soft curve of Ashley's shoulders and kissed the hollow of her neck.

The touch of Justin's lips was a delicious sensation to Ashley. She leaned against the luxurious softness of the throw and looked up at him through thick lashes. "Thank you."

"Thank you for the wrap or thank you for the kiss?" His gaze was as soft as his kiss.

"Both." Her body ached for more of his touch.

"I wrap up in this throw when I want to sit out here and look at the view on cool days." Justin's gaze traveled over her face and searched her eyes.

After the last remnants of the sun had set, Justin took Ashley's hand and walked with her inside. "I have something to ask you."

A slow smile crossed Ashley's face. "What do you want to know?"

They sat down on the sofa. Justin moved closer to Ashley. His eyes gleamed like glassy volcanic rock. "I've told you before how I feel about you." He wrapped his arm around her shoulders. "I can't get you out of my mind, Ashley." He took her hand in his and kissed it softly. "Ashley, I want you to be my girlfriend. Will you see me exclusively?"

Ashley nervously touched the base of her neck, turning her head away. She feared committing fully to a serious relationship with Justin or anyone else, because of her fear of winding up with a man like her father.

Justin could read Ashley's mind. "You're afraid I'll be like your father. Aren't you?"

Justin remembered stopping her father from stabbing her mother with a fork. He knew that kind of violence had affected Ashley. As the first man in Ashley's life, Justin knew that her father had set the mold for what Ashley expected in a romantic relationship. He knew that Ashley might have reservations about committing to him, and so he'd prepared his heart for her rejection.

Holding his breath, he raised his eyebrows, offering Ashley a questioning gaze. "You can be honest with me."

Ashley took her time to think as she fought a battle inside her soul. Swallowing hard, she turned her head to face Justin. Her eyes brimmed with tenderness and passion. "You're nothing like my father." She'd caught herself in time to fathom that Justin had shown no signs of being anything like her father. He'd been nothing but kind and loving to her. She felt completely protected and happy with Justin. She resisted the urge to revert to her noncommittal, evasive ways. She decided to take a leap of faith.

"Yes, Justin. I'll be your girlfriend."

Justin pulled the ring box out of his pocket. "Will you wear this to represent my love for you?" He opened up the box.

Ashley's eyes widened at the brilliant solitaire diamond ring. "I will."

Justin lifted her left hand to his lips and kissed it softly. He slid the ring on her third finger. "Come here Baby," he whispered into her ear.

Justin wrapped his arms around her, holding her snugly. His mouth covered hers in a kiss that was slow and thoughtful. Ashley melted in his embrace. Her body tingled from his touch, firm and persuasive, inviting more. His kisses sent the pit of her stomach into a wild swirl. She kissed him with a hunger that belied her outward calm.

He lifted her up from the sofa into his strong arms and carried her into his bedroom. He gently eased her down onto the bed. She softly moaned as he lay her down. He slid his hands under her blouse across her silken belly. He lifted her blouse above her head and slid his hands across her lacy bra.

Ashley curved into his body caressing the length of his back. His hands slipped inside the waistline of her shorts, unzipping them. Ashley removed her shorts and her bra. Justin removed his clothes, tossing them haphazardly across the room. He stood above her in all of his glory watching as Ashley lay naked beneath his gaze. Ashley gasped as bare chest met bare chest. Justin sensed the awakening flames within Ashley. He guided her hand around his waist. He caressed her full breasts budded with brown peaks. Ashley lay in the haven of Justin's love. Her breasts crushed against the hardness of his chest. He kissed her taut nipples, rousing a melting sweetness within her. Ashley's impatience grew to explosive proportions. Justin's expert touch sent her to even higher levels of ecstasy. Together they found the tempo that bound their bodies together. They both exploded in a downpour of fiery sensations. Contentment and peace flowed between Ashley and Justin, as they lay in each other's arms. Ashley knew she'd made the right decision. She couldn't imagine herself loving any other man on earth.

***

The next morning, Justin leaned on his elbow looking down at Ashley as she slept. He pushed a strand of stray hair away from her face. Slowly and seductively, his gaze slid downward to the silky blue sheet wrapped around her like a warm blanket. He felt like the luckiest man in the world to find the perfect woman for him. Some people spent an entire lifetime looking for their perfect match, but he'd found his.

He leaned over and kissed her neck, causing her to turn around to face him. He brushed a gentle kiss across her lips. "Wake up Baby."

A lovely moan slipped from her lips as her eyelids fluttered open. "Good morning my handsome Knight," she said gently caressing the side of his face with the palm of her hand.

He smiled at her comment.

"You don't mind if I call you my handsome Knight do you?" Happiness filled her as she spoke.

"Baby, you can call me whatever you want." His eyes raked boldly over her body. He radiated a vitality that drew her like a magnet. Her body ached for his touch. Reading her mind, he removed the sheet and pulled her into the cradle of his arms. His hand seared a path down her thigh. She felt transported on a soft and wispy cloud. She gasped as he lowered his body onto hers awakening a tingling in the pit of her stomach. Passion pounded the blood through her heart, chest, and head as waves of ecstasy throbbed through her body once again. He freed in her a bursting of sensations that left her with a deep feeling of love.

Hours later, they had breakfast on the patio. Justin's mood seemed suddenly lighthearted. All he could think about was celebrating the fact that Ashley had said yes. He exhaled a long sigh of contentment. "You've made me the happiest man in the world. I feel like celebrating. Why don't we go out dancing tonight in San Francisco?"

Ashley felt happy too. "I can't remember the last time I went out dancing. I may have forgotten the latest steps."

"Don't worry, it'll come back. My friend gave me a VIP pass to this club called Dady'O."

She paused for a moment. "Never heard of it. What kind of club is that?"

"It's the hottest club in San Francisco. They have another one in Cancun, Mexico."

"It sounds great, but I didn't bring any evening clothes."

"We can buy some at some boutiques in San Francisco."

"Why not." Ashley said laughing. "Dancing is a good stress reliever. It'll be good for our health."

"I'm not going for my health, Sweetness; I'm going to let loose and celebrate with my new girlfriend."

Joy bubbled in Ashley's laugh and shone in her eyes. "Then, I'll celebrate with my new boyfriend."

***

A blast of cool CO2 mist blew into Ashley's face from the ceiling as she and Justin walked through the cave-like architecture that led into a jammed pack Dady'O night club. Blinding colors from a laser light show and loud Hip-Hop music played in a state of the art sound system that heightened her senses. Normally she was not one for crowds, but this place felt mysterious and magical.

She saw several empty cocktail tables on multilevel platforms. A muscular man standing near the door asked Justin if he needed some help. Justin showed him the VIP pass that Hawk had given him. The buffed bouncer pointed to a private party in the VIP zone located on the edge of the dance floor near the back. Justin saw Hawk sitting at a table with some of his friends.

Smiling, Justin took Ashley by the hand and led her to a seat next to him. He sat next to Hawk.

"I see you decided to come," Hawk said, scanning Ashley's figure in her Caribbean blue sleeveless dress.

"Hawk, this is my girlfriend, Ashley. Ashley this is my good friend Hawk."

Hawk took a step back gave Justin a curious look and whispered. "Is this Ashley from Ashley's Day Spa?"

"In the flesh." Justin grinned.

"Nice to meet you Ashley." Hawk said. He introduced Justin and Ashley to his six foot five baller friends for whom he'd investigated cases involving illegal steroids. The athletes all stood up and scanned Ashley's figure hugging dress. Justin raised a skeptical brow, "Come on Ashley let's dance."

While they were dancing, Justin cut loose doing some dance moves that Ashley had never seen. They both enjoyed themselves dancing to the music. Then the music stopped. There was a problem with the sound system. They both held each other close. Then the music came back on playing a slow song by Kanye West.

"That music sounds so good," Ashley said.

"You feel good in my arms Baby."

After the music had stopped, they walked back to their seats. Justin pulled out Ashley's chair. Justin saw that Hawk and his friends were socializing on the dance floor with some ladies. The music started again. Justin spoke directly into Ashley's ear. "What kind of drink would you like?"

"I'll have a Margarita."

"Wait here, I'll be right back."

When Justin returned, he gave Ashley her margarita, and they drank and danced all night. Justin hailed a taxi to take them to the Habeas Corpus docked in Pier 31. "I just had to celebrate with you tonight."

"I enjoyed myself too," Ashley said with hooded eyes."

They both went into Justin's stateroom where the Habeas Corpus rocked them to sleep.

The next morning, Justin looked at Ashley sleeping and thought she had a childlike innocence about her. He began to think about his childhood. He thought about the day his grandmother gave him the nickname, "the strong one." He felt ten feet tall when she called him that. He was the one that his family turned to for strength and guidance, especially in a crisis. He identified completely with this role. He felt that to give it up would be to lose his identity. He felt like his well-being and survival depended on fulfilling this role in life. He had to be the strong one. His grandmother had all of the qualities associated with what he wished his mother could be; warm, caring, nurturing, approving, gentle, and sensitive. He realized that Ashley had all of those traits.

Ashley's cell phone rang pulling Justin out of his thoughts and waking Ashley out of a deep sleep. Ashley rolled over in bed finding herself tangled up in the navy Hermes cashmere blanket while Justin looked on. With a sigh, she reached for her cell phone that she'd placed on the nightstand next to her. It was the spa.

"India and Christina are fighting again," Amara complained.

Ashley heard loud voices in the background. She raised herself up in the bed and leaned against the headboard. "Any customer's there yet?"

"Not yet."

"Good. I'll be in as soon as I can." She turned off her cell phone.

"What's the matter?" Justin asked, leaning on an elbow, looking into her face.

Ashley looked into his eyes and smiled.

"Nothing."

"I can tell by your conversation that something is wrong. Tell me." Before he could finish his question, her cell phone rang again.

It was Le, the manicurist and Jennifer, the esthetician, on Le's speaker phone. Le spoke with a loud voice. "We are leaving the spa. Too much fighting."

Jennifer chimed in with Le and said. "Ashley, we can't work here any longer Christina and India have lost their minds. They fight all the time, but they don't do it in front of you."

Ashley swung her legs on the side of the bed. She lowered her head into her palms and bottled up her feelings. "Okay, Jennifer." Their fighting that was now interfering with her weekend getaway.

"What happened?" Justin asked.

"Christina and India are at it again. Le and Jennifer just quit," she said with a nonchalant tone.

Justin read Ashley's body language and listened to her laidback voice. He felt like she was in denial. He saw Ashley brush Christina and India's fighting under the rug as if they'd never fought before. Why was Ashley acting like nothing was wrong, now that two of her best workers had just quit.

She looked up at Justin with hooded eyes and

said, "Don't worry."

A red flag went up in Justin's mind when people said "don't worry". To Justin—that meant he better worry. He knew that Ashley was in trouble and unable to deal with the hostility going on at her spa. His instinct to help Ashley kicked in. He decided right then and there to be her strength in this situation.

***

When Ashley arrived at the spa, Le and Jennifer had packed up their belongings and left. Ashley walked into her office, ignoring Christina and India, and placed an online advertisement for a manicurist and esthetician. She would deal with Christina and India later.

Chapter 11

The next day, Justin had to meet his client at one o'clock for the reading of the equal pay verdict.

Justin and Heather Jones, stood up in the hot, crowded courtroom. The female jury foreman, stood up and read the verdict. "We the jury, find the defendant, The City of Sunrise, California, not guilty of the charge of equal pay discrimination." News reporters burst through the doors into the hallway to meet waiting cameramen. Justin looked stunned as the jury leader read the verdict. There were more women than men on the jury. He couldn't understand why the women jury members didn't ban together and vote in their own interest. He'd worked hard during the jury selection process to ensure there were more women than men. But now in hindsight, he realized the importance of choosing the right women.

Lights flashed into Justin's eyes and those of his high profile client, as they exited the courtroom.

A reporter stuck a microphone in Justin's face. "How does it feel to lose this high-profile equal pay case for your client?"

"My client and I both feel that justice has not been served today. We will appeal the case."

As a civil rights attorney, Justin had won

numerous civil rights cases, involving sexual discrimination, equal pay, wrongful death and domestic violence.

Another reporter stuck a microphone in Justin's face. "What does this decision mean for equal pay?"

Justin's jaw twitched as he spoke. "This verdict is a setback for equal pay for women. Unfortunately, we can't control a jury's decision. We will appeal the case."

"Does your client have anything to say?"

"My client has no comment," Justin said. "Excuse me." He made his way through the crowd protecting his client from the media.

Justin escorted Heather out of the courthouse to her car and waited for her to drive off. His friend Hawk caught up with him in the parking lot.

"I'm sorry about your loss. I'm starving. Let's go get some lunch. My treat," Hawk offered.

"I'm not hungry Hawk." Justin wanted to be alone in his office.

"I still can't believe the jury ruled in favor of the employer. There were more women than men on that jury." Hawk shook his head. "Some people don't seem to care about their own interests. Too bad your client will get paid a lower wage than the men performing the same job."

"The sad part is many female employees are unaware that they are experiencing violations of these equal pay laws."

"Yeah, that's sad Justin." Hawk said rubbing his stomach.

"I'll appeal the case though. The loss of this case is only round one." Justin lowered his head giving Hawk a bitter smile. "My client deserved to win her case," Skin bunched around Justin's eyes as he stared painfully into Hawk's face. He could kick himself for losing. He hated to lose.

***

A male courier delivered an envelope requiring a signature to the receptionist's desk at the spa.

"I need a signature for this letter." The messenger said.

Amara looked at the letter and thought it looked important. "Please wait while I get the owner."

Ashley came out of her office and signed the letter. After opening it, she saw that it was a personal injury lawsuit naming Ashley's Day Spa as the defendant. Kimberly Lewis, the plaintiff, was suffering from a neck injury caused by a massage at the spa.

Ashley and Christina were the only masseuses at the spa. Ashley's mouth went dry. She tried to think, but the plaintiff's name didn't ring a bell. She'd never met anyone named Kimberly Lewis. She picked up the appointment book and took it with her to her office.

"Everything okay?" Amara's eyes clung to Ashley's when Ashley removed the appointment book.

"I'll bring it right back. I want to check something." Ashley walked away from Amara. "I'll be in my office if anyone needs me."

Ashley plopped onto her white leather sofa in the corner. Crossing her legs, she leaned back on her sofa and continued to read the document. The plaintiff was claiming damages in the amount of $250,000. She looked at the date of injury and saw that it occurred while she was uninsured. Ashley's eyes widened.

She picked up her cell phone and called her attorney. The receptionist answered the phone informing Ashley that her attorney no longer worked there.

"What happened?"

"He was disbarred."

"Disbarred? Why was he disbarred?"

"You have to talk to someone else about that Ms. Jacobs. Michael Gordon is handling all of his cases." The receptionist added.

"May I speak with Mr. Gordon? I'm calling about a lawsuit."

"He hasn't come in yet. I can have him call you when he arrives."

"Is he available this afternoon?"

"Yes, his schedule is open all day."

"Good. I'll bring in the paperwork this afternoon." Ashley ended her call.

Moments later Christina stuck her head inside Ashley's open door. "Hey, Ashley. Is anything wrong?"

Ashley looked up from the legal document. "I'm glad you stopped by Chris. I have a question."

Christina walked in and sat next to Ashley.

"I received this lawsuit today. Kimberly Lewis claims that you injured her neck during a massage. Does the name ring a bell?"

"No. I don't recall that name."

"I checked the appointment book and saw that you gave Ms. Lewis a neck massage on the date that she claims her injury occurred at the spa."

"I'm sorry, Ashley, but I have a ton of

customers. I can't remember all of their names."

"Yeah, so do I. Thanks, Christina. I just wanted to find out if you remembered her."

Normally, Ashley would be forced to fire a worker for injuring a client, but since Christina was her best friend, Ashley decided to wait to see what happened in this case before doing anything drastic.

Christina looked at her watch. "Ash. I have a client coming in for a full body massage in a few minutes. Anything else?"

"No. That's all." Ashley continued to read through the legal document. Christina walked back to the massage room to wait for her client.

***

At twelve noon, Ashley walked into the law offices of Bryan, Foyle & Chan and greeted the young attractive receptionist.

"Good afternoon, I called earlier this morning. I have some papers for Mr. Jeremy Gordon."

"Have a seat. He'll be out in a minute."

Ashley sat down in a cognac hued leather armchair in the waiting area. She looked around and saw that the pale blue walls were a perfect canvas to display the muted tones in the landscape artwork.

A young man with red hair and green eyes came up to Ashley. He looked no more than twenty.

"Ms. Jacobs? I'm Jeremy Gordon. Please follow me." They walked into a conference room and sat around a small conference table surrounded by black leather chairs.

Ashley handed him the letter."

"I'll have my secretary make a copy of this before you go." He said.

After talking to him for about an hour, Ashley found out that he had just graduated from law school. She hoped he had enough experience to handle her case.

"Let me look this over. Once I've read it, I'll give you a call."

"Can you call me today?"

"I'll try."

Ashley stood up, shook his hand and went back to the spa.

***

After Ashley had finished her appointments, she sat in her office waiting for Mr. Gordon to call. Her phone rang. It was Mr. Gordon's office.

"Ms. Jacobs."

"Yes."

"I've read over your lawsuit and I recommend that you settle out of court with the plaintiff."

"Why do you think I should settle?"

"Because the plaintiff has some serious injuries, and you run the risk of a jury awarding the plaintiff more than $250,000."

"Can you write up the settlement?"

"No problem Ms. Jacobs. I'll write up the settlement agreement and get back with you."

"Thank you, Mr. Gordon."

"You're welcome."

Ashley placed the receiver down and began looking through her bank account records on her computer. This settlement was going to set back her plans for expanding the spa.

Chapter 12

Instead of staying at home licking his wounds, Justin worked on his appeal.

Hours later, Justin's thoughts shifted to his weekend with Ashley. They'd made love all night long. There was nothing that he wouldn't do for Ashley. He admitted that he was in love. For the first time in his life, he'd found a woman that he wanted to marry.

He thought about romantic places where he could propose marriage. Maybe on The Habeas Corpus while they pleasure cruised in the bay. She seemed to enjoy sailing with him. Maybe beneath the Golden Gate Bridge before sailing out into the Pacific Ocean. It didn't matter to him where he proposed as long as she said yes.

He looked at his watch and saw that it was five o'clock. She'd be off work in another hour. He wanted to see her tonight. He had not called her this morning because he didn't want to crowd her. He decided to call her before he left the office for the day.

At five o'clock, Justin called Ashley on his cell phone to see if she would go out to dinner with him.

Ashley looked at the screen on her ringing cell phone and saw that it was Justin.

"Hey, Sweetness, you want to have dinner with me tonight?"

"Hi, Justin. No, I'm not hungry." Ashley hadn't eaten anything all day.

"Well then, can I come over tonight?"

"No. That's not a good idea either."

"Why?"

"I have too much on my mind."

"What's on your mind, Baby?"

"I'm being sued for $250,000, and I have to pay it out of my pocket."

"What do you mean you have to pay it out of your pocket? Don't you have liability insurance?" He quickly pointed out.

"No... I mean yes... I mean, the injury occurred after my insurance had lapsed." She said calmly."

"What happened?"

"Someone misplaced my insurance bill, and so it lapsed."

Justin wondered how Ashley could be so irresponsible to allow her liability insurance to lapse, especially in her line of business. What was she thinking?

Ashley intuitively read Justin's mind. "I never saw the bill until it was too late. I tried to pay it the same day that I found it, but the policy had lapsed."

"Don't you know when your bills are due? I mean weren't you looking for the bill?"

"I pay my bills as soon as I receive them. I should have asked to receive my insurance bill online, and then none of this would have happened. But I used snail mail to receive my insurance bill instead." Ashley could tell by Justin's silence, that he wanted to hear more. She continued to defend herself. "Things were so hectic around here with India and Christina arguing and fighting, that the insurance bill slipped my mind."

Justin understood her explanation. "Now tell me more about this lawsuit?"

"It's a personal injury lawsuit naming my spa as the defendant. The plaintiff, Kimberly Lewis is suffering from a neck injury caused by a massage at the spa several weeks ago." Ashley thought back to her conversation with Christina. "Ms. Lewis was one of Christina's customers, but Christina doesn't remember having Kimberly Lewis as a client." She continued. "Ms. Lewis was injured after my old insurance policy had lapsed. So that's why I have to pay the damages out of my pocket," She said evenly.

"Do you have the money?" Justin asked.

"Of course I do. I have extra reserves in a contingency fund. I'll have to put off expanding my spa for a while."

What alarmed Justin was that Ashley's voice didn't match the seriousness of her situation. He knew she would need a good attorney. "Tell me about your attorney. Who do you have representing you?"

"The law offices of Bryan, Foyle & Chan. But my attorney has been disbarred. Mr. Jeremy Gordon is handling my case."

Justin knew the law firm. They were ambulance-chasers. "Why was your attorney disbarred? What's his name?"

"His name is Michael Foyle. They wouldn't tell me why."

"Hum, I know Michael." Justin had heard Michael was disbarred for lying in court. "What did Mr. Gordon say about your case?"

"He advised me to settle out of court." Ashley said with a calm voice.

"What!" Her lawyer hadn't even had enough time to research the evidence. How could he come to that decision? "Baby. I didn't know you were going through a lawsuit. Why didn't you tell me?"

"I didn't tell you because my attorney said he

was going to handle the settlement."

Justin could tell that her attorney was a greenhorn. "Did he tell you that a personal injury lawsuit could affect the reputation of your spa? Your customers would be afraid to come to your spa for treatments."

"No. We never discussed that possibility."

Justin believed that Ashley's attorney was too inexperienced to handle her case. She could lose her business behind his incompetence. "Are you at home?" Justin asked abruptly.

"Yes."

"I'm on my way. I'll be right over."

***

Justin drove into Ashley's driveway thirty minutes later. She opened the door and appeared to be distracted. She had a listless look in her eyes. He kissed her lips, but her kiss was nothing like her passionate kisses in Sausalito.

In a protective gesture, he took her hand and walked with her to the sofa. He looked into her eyes and said, "I'm here for you Baby."

"Things seem to be falling apart Justin." Ashley said calmly. Whenever her problems disturbed her peace of mind, she disassociated herself from them, and turned a blind eye to her feelings.

"Where's your document?" Justin asked.

Ashley brought her briefcase out of her bedroom and handed him the document.

Justin looked it over thoroughly. A red flag went up in his mind when he saw Christina's name. He didn't trust her—he smelled fraud. Justin gave Ashley a piercing look. "Even if you have to pay the damages out of your pocket, your attorney should have explained that your standing as a reputable spa owner would be ruined." Justin gave her a serious look. "You could lose your business Ashley. I think you should fire your attorney and let me handle your case."

"Fire my attorney?" Her eyes were pools of appeal.

"Yes. Your attorney is lazy and inexperienced. To put it bluntly, he's taking the easy way out." You have a major problem on your hands, and you need a good lawyer."

Ashley perked up as she listened to Justin. She trusted his advice more than she trusted Mr. Gordon's.

"You can't treat these kinds of things lightly. You need to make some serious decisions." Justin looked into Ashley's eyes and saw that listless look had faded away. She was back to her sweet self.

"You know what you need?" He wanted to say she needed some good loving, but he couldn't tell her that after what she'd been through today. "You need some rest. You've been through a lot today." He stood up. "Now walk me to the door and give me a hug. I'll talk to you about your case tomorrow. Don't worry Baby. I've got your back."

Ashley's smile broadened in approval. She felt a bottomless peace and satisfaction after talking to Justin. Like a modern day knight in shining armor, Justin helped her in her time of need. She kissed him passionately as she spoke between kisses. "Thank you for taking my case Justin."

Justin returned her kisses with his last words smothered on her lips. "No problem, Sweetness." All of his life, Justin's identified with his role as *the strong one*. Now, Ashley needed Justin's strength as much as he needed her peaceful spirit. Stepping away, he touched her chin with his thumb. "Get some sleep." He turned around and left.

Chapter 13

Christina lay in her bed whispering on her cell phone with Kimberly Lewis. Bradford turned around to listen.

"Put her on the speaker phone," Bradford said, suspecting that Christina was hiding something.

Christina pressed the speaker button. "Have you heard anything about the lawsuit?" Christina asked.

"My attorney is asking for $250,000 in damages. We can split the money three ways." Kimberly said.

Bradford sat up. "Your lawyer has to take his fees out first."

"Before his fees are taken out, we will each get eighty-three thousand dollars," Christina said.

Christina met Bradford at a bar when he was an unemployed barber. She recommended him to Ashley when Ashley was looking to hire a barber for the spa. Christina fell for Bradford because he was muscular. She loved a man with muscles. By the time Christina had met Bradford, she was ripe for taking her jealousy out on Ashley.

Bradford and Kimberly had plotted with

Christina to set up a fraudulent personal injury lawsuit against Ashley's spa. Bradford had told Christina that that Ashley's malpractice insurance would pay for the damages. Christina went along with the plot. India and the other ladies at the spa suspected that Christina was jealous of Ashley, but they remained silent because they knew Ashley was in denial about Christina's friendship and they wanted to keep their jobs.

Since Christina and Ashley first met in the seventh grade, Christina grew jealous of Ashley's beauty and shapely body. Christina had plain facial features and a stout body. As the years passed, Christina's jealousy grew. She tried to dress like Ashley in high school to attract boys, but it didn't work. The student body had voted for Ashley as *The Nicest Girl*. Christina was barely recognized by the student body. When they both went to college, Christina struggled with her classes while Ashley flourished. Christina began to work for Ashley's Spa soon after it opened. Christina's jealousy of Ashley grew with every passing day, especially when she saw Ashley's business prosper.

She turned to Bradford. "What are you going to do with your money?"

"I'm going to pay off my daughter's doctor's bills," he said. "She needs to have an operation for a hole in her heart." Leaning back on the headboard, he rubbed her arm and asked. "What are you going to do with yours?"

"I'm going to buy a new wardrobe and take a long vacation. Maybe a cruise around the Caribbean. Want to come?"

"No. I don't have time for that." Bradford said.

"What about you Kimberly. What are you going to do with your money?" Christina asked.

"I'm going to help my boyfriend produce his rap CD."

Kimberly got the idea of insurance fraud from her brother, who was just released from prison.

***

Justin sat on the side of his bed scrolling through his cell phone emails. He hadn't slept well last night. He had recurring nightmares that someone in Ashley's spa was behind that lawsuit. He called Ashley on his cell phone.

"Good morning, Justin." Ashley said as she stretched out her arms and yawned.

"Morning, Baby. Before I go to work, I want to ask you a question."

"Sure."

"I'd like to install surveillance cameras in your spa."

"What? You can't do that. It would be an

invasion of privacy for my clients."

"Don't worry, we'll place the cameras in strategic locations. Your clients will not have their privacy invaded. It's only to find out what your workers are saying and doing while you're not there."

"I don't know, Justin."

"I think someone inside your spa might be behind your lawsuit."

"What? Why would someone want to do that?"

"Trust me, Baby. I've seen people do worse. You'd be surprised by the things people do."

"Okay. If you think so."

"I'm going to need a set of your keys."

"Alright. I have an extra set."

"Good. I'll try to get Hawk to install the cameras tonight after everyone has left. I'll come by and get your keys later today."

"Okay."

Justin ended the call and immediately called Hawk.

Hawk leaned back in his faded brown leather office chair blowing smoke rings into the air. He was dead tired. Today was a good day to kick back and rest between jobs. Crime around the Bay Area was getting so bad that private citizens kept him busy day and night investigating cases especially involving motel rooms and cheating spouses.

In high school, Hawk and Justin played on the high school football team together. UCLA had drafted Hawk in his senior year, but he suffered a leg injury and decided to become a licensed private investigator like his father. Hawk's cell phone rang.

"Hawk, this is Justin."

"What's up?"

"I have some work for you."

"And good morning to you, too!" Hawk said sarcastically. "You can't greet a brother good morning anymore?"

"I'm sorry. I just have a lot on my mind."

"What kind of work?"

"Ashley is being sued. I need you to do a background check on the plaintiff. I also need you to install surveillance cameras in Ashley's spa."

Hawk lowered his feet from his desk and listened attentively. "Surveillance cameras and a background check huh. Sounds interesting." He leaned on his elbows holding the phone between his ear and shoulder as he smashed the butt of his cigarette in a paper cup. "What's the plaintiff's name?"

"Her name is Kimberly Lewis."

"Okay, I'll check on her."

"Something doesn't pass the smell test in Ashley's lawsuit," Justin said.

"Why do you think that?"

"You know I can smell a fraud a mile away. I think someone in Ashley's spa is trying to get money out of her insurance company. But they don't know that Ashley wasn't covered during the injury. Ashley has to pay damages out of her pocket."

"Why don't you call the police?"

"I can't let the police or the media find out about this personal injury case. It would ruin the reputation of Ashley's spa. We need to fly under the radar while we investigate this case. I also need you to follow one of her workers and take photos. So, can you keep this investigation quiet?"

"You know it. I'll start on the background check this morning. When do you want me to install the cameras?"

"Any time after ten tonight when the spa is closed. I have a set of keys that I'll give you. I'll meet you over there tonight at ten." Justin ended the call and prepared to go into his office.

Hawk performed a background check on Kimberly D. Lewis and found she had a rap sheet three pages long. He found out that she'd filed numerous lawsuits all over the country, and had been convicted of credit card fraud and check cashing scams in multiple states. She'd been evicted from apartments numerous times and had a brother who served prison time for insurance fraud and bad checks.

Late that night, Justin and Hawk opened the door to the spa and installed surveillance cameras in every room. Justin pointed to places where Hawk should install cameras.

"We now have views of Ashley's spa on my closed circuit TV's in my office," Hawk said.

***

Early the next morning, Hawk sat in his black Buick Regal outside Christina's house and waited for her to leave. She came out with Bradford. Hawk took photos of them entering a white Chevy Camero. He took photos of them driving away. He followed them and took photos of them entering into the spa. He sat in his car outside the spa and waited for them to leave.

When they came out for lunch, Hawk tailed them to a local bar. He watched them meet with a young woman who he suspected was Kimberly Lewis. He immediately took photos of all three living it up in the bar. These photos will prove that they are all in cahoots, he thought.

But first, he had to find out if the woman was Kimberly Lewis. He walked inside to get close up shots of them. He stood in a doorway separating the bar from the restaurant taking photos with his telephoto zoom lens. He heard Christina call the woman Kim. Suddenly Bradford looked up and spotted Hawk.

Hawk walked quickly through the restaurant into the kitchen and out the back door. Bradley caught up with him in the parking lot.

"Hey, man. I saw you taking photos of me. What's up?"

Hawk's eyes looked like those of a hawk. Hawk sized up Bradford and determined that he was stronger. "I'm a photographer for Bar & Restaurant Magazine." Hawk dared Bradford to ask another question with his piercing look. Hawk drove back to his office, leaving Bradford standing in the driveway looking bewildered. Hawk was glad he got some good close up shots of all three of them because he knew he wouldn't get any more. Bradford was onto him.

Christina and Bradford arrived back at the spa

an hour later. They both met in the massage room. They were unaware that every word they said was being recorded on videotape. Hawk installed a hidden camera behind a wall sconce near the massage table.

"I don't think that guy today was from a magazine. I think he was from Ashley's insurance company."

"I don't think so," Christina said.

"Why not?"

"Because Ashley let her insurance lapse. When Kim came in for her massage, the spa wasn't covered." Christina said.

"Well, how are we going to get paid if Ashley's insurance won't cover the damages?" Bradford asked.

"Out of her pocket!" Christina said angrily. "Ashley lives off of her business and a trust fund she inherited from her grandfather. I want to get her where it hurts the most—in her bank account."

Chapter 14

Justin arrived at Ashley's house at seven o'clock in the evening. One week had passed since Hawk had installed the cameras in the spa. Justin had a boat load of evidence to prove that Christina, Bradford, and Kimberly were behind the fraudulent lawsuit. He had photos of Kimberly performing normal physical activities without wearing a neck brace, proving her injuries were a fraud. He also had photos of Christina, Bradford and Kimberly partying together at that same bar, proving they all knew each other.

Ashley sat on the sofa next to Justin, wearing her work uniform. Justin spread out photos of Christina, Bradford and Kimberly on the coffee table.

"These photos were taken last week."

Ashley looked at the photos and said nothing.

Justin continued. "These photos prove that Christina, Bradford and Kimberly all know each other. I think they are behind your lawsuit."

Ashley looked at the photos and gave Justin a look of disbelief. She turned her head away and said nothing.

Justin pulled out his cell phone and played a

video taken from a surveillance camera. "This video was taken last Wednesday." Justin lowered his head. "It proves that they all initially wanted to commit insurance fraud against your spa. Now that your insurance has lapsed, they are coming after your assets."

"Justin, I hear what you're saying." She closed her eyes, her heart aching with pain. "It's just... give me some time." She needed more time to ease the pain.

"You don't have any time Ashley. These people are taking you to court."

"I understand that, but I need to do this my way."

Justin had enough evidence to prove that Christina was no real friend of Ashley's. He had no intention of telling Ashley that Christina had brazenly flirted with him at her spa. He knew that Ashley was in denial about her friendship with Christina. The only way he knew how to fight denial was with facts. He told her about Christina in an indirect way. "Some people smile in your face and stab you in your back."

"How could Christina do this to me?" Ashley pressed her hands over her face convulsively to hide her eyes from the video.

Justin pulled her hands away from her face. "I know it's painful to watch, Ashley, but the video proves that, Kimberly Lewis is clearly not injured. It also proves that Christina, Bradford, and Kimberly set you up." He lowered his head, shaking it regretfully.

Ashley watched the video of Kimberly carrying bags of groceries into her house. She watched Kimberly dancing at a night club, and then one of her exercising at a Zumba class. Kimberly wasn't wearing her neck brace during any of these activities. She watched and listened as Christina and Bradford talked about getting money from Ashley.

"I just can't believe it."

"Evidence doesn't lie." Justin paused looking Ashley in the eye. "Fraud is a felony offense. This evidence can send them to prison."

Ashley's body posture slumped while she calmly watched the video, rubbing her eyes. "Why would my best friend, want to sue me?" She could no longer control her own anger and pain. "I have to know. I've known Christina since we were kids. Why would she betray me like this?"

"Christina can answer that question better than anyone else."

Ashley stiffened, crossing her arms. "I'm going to ask her why."

Justin held out the palm of his hand in a gesture to stop Ashley. "I don't think you should communicate with Christina any further," Justin advised. He wanted to handle Christina himself because not only had she committed a serious crime, but she could be dangerous, now that there was evidence against her. He didn't think Ashley was equipped to handle a person like Christina.

Ashley gave him a determined look. "Trust me. I can handle Christina."

Justin's jaw tightened. Usually, he was a self-restrained, patient person. But when pushed, he could turn into an openly aggressive and domineering man. He needed to feel that Ashley was behind him, supporting his efforts. If she refused, he knew he had a tendency to become confrontational and unwilling to back down. This little ping pong dance with Ashley was causing him to become frustrated. He knew if given a chance, Christina would only exploit Ashley's friendship and make her case worse.

He leaned forward, and said in a controlling voice. "Ashley, I can't help you if you won't let me help you. You must stand behind me and let me handle Christina. She is a major player in your lawsuit. You don't want to complicate your case."

"Complicate my case. How can I complicate my case, just by asking her why she did it?"

"By giving Christina a chance to manipulate you. I think you are in denial about Christina's motives. If you contact her, all she is going to do is play you like a violin."

"I've known Christina since I was thirteen. If anyone knows her, it's me. Not you."

Justin couldn't take Ashley's denial any longer. She refused to stand behind him and let him do his job. She had finally pushed his button. He spoke with a critical tone in his voice. "Your mother was right. Your head is in the clouds. You can't handle Christina. She's a crook! I see people like her every day. I see people for who they are, not who I want them to be."

Ashley refused to plug into Justin's insults. "You know how much I hate those words," Ashley said calmly. Justin's domineering attitude reminded her of her father. Her worst fear surfaced. What if Justin turned out to be as abusive as her father? She clammed up at the thought, and Justin's harsh tone only made things worse. Standing up she said, "You're just as abusive and domineering as my father. I don't think our relationship is going to work out, Justin."

Justin watched her trying to take his ring off of her swollen finger.

"Keep it," he said, standing up. "There's no convincing you to let me do my job. I'll talk to you later." He walked out of her house.

Ashley fell on her sofa and cried herself to sleep.

At midnight, Ashley woke up out of a dream. All she could see was Justin's face and that video repeatedly playing over in her mind. She sat up on her sofa and stared at the photos for a long time. Leaning back on the sofa, she thought back to when her mother said those painful words to her. Her father had blacked her mother's eye in a fight that Ashley had broken up. Ashley went outside and sat in a rocking chair on the back porch. Her mother came out while Ashley was looking up at the sky. Ashley had asked her mother why she didn't leave her father. Ashley remembered like it was yesterday. Her mother told her to, "Get your head out of the clouds. Women have to put up with abusive relationships to survive, especially when there is no place else for them to go." Ashley believed her mother then. But those days were over. Now, there were women's shelters everywhere for victims of domestic abuse. Tears rolled down Ashley's face. She believed her mother should have left her father especially after her brother died. Then her mind turned back to Justin. He was right.

Suddenly, from somewhere deep inside Ashley's soul, her anger surfaced. For the first time in her life, she wasn't afraid to face conflict. She realized how blind she'd been. She was angry at herself for running Justin away. He had tried hard to get her to open her eyes and let him handle Christina. She looked at the photos for a long time. She got her head out of the clouds and realized the truth. She'd always suspected that Christina wasn't her true friend. But she was in denial for years, sweeping Christina's behavior under the rug. But now, Ashley wanted answers. She was going to confront Christina with the photos and ask her one question. Why.

The next morning, Ashley called Christina on her cell phone.

"Christina, got any plans for today?"

"No, just a lazy Sunday kicking it with Bradford."

"Why don't you guys come over for lunch? My treat."

"That sounds good. What time?"

"About noon."

"Okay. We'll be there."

Twelve noon came quickly. Ashley opened a bottle of wine and prepared some sandwiches.

Christina and Bradford knocked on her door. "Hey, you guys. Come on in and have a glass of wine." She'd deliberately left the photos on the coffee table.

Christina sat down on the sofa and saw the photos. Bradford saw the photos and excused himself to use the restroom.

Ashley walked out of her kitchen holding two glasses of red wine. She handed one to Christina and placed Bradford's glass on the coffee table. Ashley went back to the kitchen and returned with her wine glass and sat next to Christina.

"What are these?" Christina asked, looking on the coffee table.

"Those are photos of you, Bradford and Kimberly Lewis having drinks together at a bar. You remember Kimberly Lewis, the woman suing me for an injured neck." Ashley stared directly into Christina's eyes. "I thought you said you didn't know Kimberly."

"I...um, I don't know her." Christina lied.

"I just want to know why you betrayed me Christina. Photos don't lie." She held a photo up to Christina's face. "Take a closer look." She paused. "These photos and a video tape Justin took of you and Bradford talking about getting money from me are enough evidence to send all three of you to prison for a long time."

Christina stood up. "I'm not listening to your threats." She spoke loudly. "Bradford. Let's go." Bradford rushed out of the bathroom.

They both left, slamming the door. Ashley stood there fuming with her hands on her hips. Christina hadn't answered Ashley's question. She picked up her phone and called Christina.

No, answer. She tossed her cell phone on the sofa next to her handbag, picked up her car keys, and rushed through the door. She jumped into her car and drove over to Christina's house.

Chapter 15

Ashley drove on a deserted road near downtown Napa's historic district where Christina lived. Suddenly the earth trembled under Ashley's car. She immediately put her car into park. A large piece of concrete fell on top of her hood. "What!" she shouted out. Then a second piece of concrete fell onto her roof. Suddenly, pieces of concrete tumbled down on the side of her car from the overpass. She rolled up her windows to keep the dust from flying inside her car. Concrete began falling in large and small chunks from the foundation of the highway overpass. She thought she was going to die.

Within minutes, her car was surrounded with concrete blocking out all sunlight. She tried to open her car door in the darkness, but it wouldn't move. She was trapped. Finally, the earthquake stopped. There was an eerie silence all around her. After a few minutes, she heard the sound of fire engines.

Stunned, Ashley sat completely still. Then her lips began to tremble. The color drained from her face as she faced the stark reality of her situation. Fortunately, the falling concrete hadn't crushed the roof of her car. She rolled down her window just enough so that the dust and pieces of concrete wouldn't come inside. "Help," she screamed out with tears welling in her eyes. But no one heard her cry. "Calm down, Ashley, you can deal with this," she said out loud. "Think."

She reached for her handbag and then remembered that she'd left it at home. She was in such a hurry to catch up with Christina that she'd picked up her car keys, and left her handbag and cell phone on the sofa.

She slapped her hand to her forehead. What was she going to do to survive this tragedy? She refused to give up and wait to be rescued by the fire department. Justin had told her not to communicate with Christina. She wouldn't be in this situation if she would have listened to him. She began to think of ways to get out of this situation. She knew she had some tire changing tools in the trunk of her car. Maybe if she could get to some of her tools, she could push away some of the concrete. She climbed over the front seat and lowered the backseat armrest that opened up to the trunk. She reached through the hole back there and felt her safety kit that contained a flashlight, bottled water, and other emergency equipment. Then she felt a crowbar and pulled it through the hole along with the safety kit.

She climbed back over the front seat, rolled down the window a bit, and began hitting the concrete with the straight end of the crowbar. Maybe someone would hear her or maybe she could dig her way out.

She worked with the crowbar for over an hour making little progress. She wished she would have listened to Justin and stayed at home. All she could do now was continue using the crowbar to make a path. She took a break, taking a sip of the bottled water from the emergency kit.

Before the earthquake, Ashley had run Justin off over her stubborn attitude. Being stuck in this situation made Ashley realize how fragile life could be. She realized how much she loved Justin, and how wrong she'd been.

***

Justin was sitting in his office downtown Napa, thinking about what to ordering from the café next door for lunch. Normally, he didn't work on Sundays, but he'd decided to go into the office today, to finish some work that was piling up. He thought about buying a big bouquet of roses from the corner florist to make up with Ashley.

Suddenly the building began to sway. The building must have swayed sideways for about two minutes. He ran out into the hall, but the elevator wouldn't work, so he exited the swaying building by walking down the stairwell.

Once outside he took a quick glance at his building and saw that there was no foundation damage. It had been retrofitted years ago to withstand earthquakes. Looking up at the gray sky, he listened closely and heard no birds chirping or street sounds, then he heard the sound of fire engines. He looked around and saw bricks, concrete and other debris scattered all over the riverfront sidewalk. Toppled flowers from the florist's shop and shattered plate glass from the coffee shop covered the sidewalk. People were walking, some running to get to their loved ones.

The only thoughts Justin had were of Ashley and his family. He called Ashley, but her cell phone went into voice mail. He called his grandmother and found out that she was fine. He called his brother's and sister and found out that they were okay. Kenton complained about bottles of wine crashing onto the floors in several of the warehouses.

Justin looked down the street and saw the driver for the corner florist run outside. The driver began picking up toppled water containers, and loose flowers scattered in front of the building.

"Everybody okay over there?" Justin asked.

"Yes. We're all inside cleaning up the mess," he said as he picked up empty flower pots, water containers, and flowers.

"Good. Let me check on everyone at Andy's café." Justin took a few steps to the café.

He stuck his head through the door. "Andy! You okay?" Justin yelled out.

"I'm fine, Justin."

Justin saw the owner peek through an opening to the kitchen.

"Just a little shaken that's all, but thanks for checking on me."

Justin walked three doors down to his brother's art gallery. He walked inside and saw the sales clerk picking up a few paintings that had fallen. He was placing them on a nearby table.

"You okay?"

"I'm fine," he said as he continued to clean up the mess.

"You talk to your brother?" the clerk asked.

"I'm getting ready to call Brandon, now," Justin said dialing his number. Brandon was okay. Next, he called Ashley's number again, but her cell phone went into voice mail.

Before the earthquake, Justin had been separated from Ashley for only one day, but it seemed like an eternity. He felt guilty for his harsh tone and for telling Ashley that she had her head in the clouds. He knew she hated those words. He didn't say them to hurt her feelings. He said them to open her eyes. He regretted it now because Ashley hadn't answered any of his calls. Since she'd refused to take his calls, he'd decided to give her some time to cool down. But now after the earthquake, he was concerned about her safety.

Standing in front of the art gallery, he left another voice mail for Ashley, indicating his concern for her safety. He hoped that she would return his call to let him know that she was okay. After an hour had passed, and she hadn't called. His heartbeat began to race, nearly exploding in his chest. He decided to drive over to Ashley's house.

On his way there, bricks and broken glass covered the streets everywhere he looked. Stop lights flashed red. People wandered in the middle of the streets. Fire engines were parked in front of businesses with sirens blasting. Police cars with flashing lights blocked the streets. Thick dust hung low in the air casting a grey shadow on everyone and everything he saw.

Through all of the chaos, Justin somehow made it through the crowded streets to Ashley's house. Once there, he rang her bell, but no answer. He used his key that she'd given him and saw her purse and cell phone lying on the sofa. He saw three full wine glasses and the photos still sitting on the coffee table. He felt in his gut, that something was wrong. Where was Ashley? He pulled out his cell phone and called Hawk.

Chapter 16

Justin was sitting on Ashley's sofa when Hawk arrived. "What took you so long?" Justin asked.

"I had to check on my family."

"Are they okay?"

"Yeah. Everyone's fine."

Justin stared at one of the photos he was holding in his hand. He looked up. "We had a fight because of these photos," He said pointing to the other photos scattered across the table. He wished he could take back every painful word he'd said to Ashley. "I have to find her." Two deep lines of worry appeared between his eyes.

"Don't worry, we'll find her," Hawk said, looking around the living room for clues. The first thing he noticed were the wine glasses. The second thing he noticed was her handbag on the sofa. "She must have been in a hurry to leave her handbag."

"I already went through it," Justin said. "She left her cell phone on the sofa, so I can't even call her."

"Did you check her cell phone calendar to see if she had plans for today?"

"Her cell phone is locked. It needs a password."

Suddenly, Ashley's cell phone rang. He saw that the call was from Cynthia Jacobs. Justin looked up at Hawk. "It's Ashley's mother." He memorized the number and called it back on his cell phone. Ashley's mother answered the phone. Justin told her not to come over to Ashley's house because she wasn't there. He continued to tell her that he was searching for her and that he would come by later today or call her as soon as he found out Ashley's location. He'd listened to her mother rant for several minutes before she ended the call.

Justin continued to look around the living room. "She had two visitors by the look of those wine glasses."

"Yeah, they didn't even bother to finish their wine or these sandwiches," Hawk said picking up a plate of sandwiches on the kitchen counter. He lifted the bread off of one of them and saw it was ham and cheese. He was about to take a bite, when he saw Justin staring at him. He put the sandwich back down and continued looking around.

"It looks like they were in a rush to leave," Justin said.

"Yeah, but the question is—why. We need to find out who was here and why they left so fast." Hawk said scratching the stubble on his chin. "They may know Ashley's whereabouts."

"Good thinking Hawk." The first two people who came to Justin's mind were Christina and

Bradford. "Maybe she invited Christina and Bradford over to show them the photos."

"Why do you think it was them?" Hawk asked walking toward the bedroom. He opened up her dresser drawer and picked up a silk nightie. Justin walked in giving him a questionable look. "I'm searching her drawers for a calendar or a journal." He said replacing the nightie. They both walked back into the living room.

"I just have a hunch it was those two," Justin said going through her wallet again. He only found cash and credit cards.

Hawk stood above him staring at the wine glasses. "If you think Christina and Bradford were the last two people who saw Ashley, then we need to talk to them. Do you know where they live?"

"No. But I can find out." Justin said picking up his cell phone. He called the spa, but then realized it was closed on Sunday's. "Come on Hawk. Let's drive over to the spa and search Ashley's files."

"Good idea. I'll meet you there," Hawk said taking one last look around.

When they arrived at the spa, they saw the closed sign on the door. There were people standing in front of the restaurant next door. "There's no sense in questioning them." Hawk said. "They won't know anything since the spa is closed."

"Let's take a look inside. We can pull Ashley's personnel files to find out where Christina and Bradley live." Justin said.

"You still have her key don't you," Hawk asked glancing at the people standing in front of the restaurant next door.

Justin reached into his pocket. "Yeah, it's right here on my key ring. Let's go inside and check out the files."

After Justin unlocked the door, they found a file cabinet in Ashley's office. Justin found a personnel file for Bradford and one for Christina. He jotted down Christina's address. He saw that Bradford's old motel address had been scratched out. His new address was the same as Christina's. "This is all I need." Justin said, closing the file cabinet. "I want to find out what they know."

"I don't think Ashley's disappearance is due to foul play."

"Why?" Justin asked.

"Because there were no signs of a struggle or broken furniture at her house." Hawk said. "I think we should go to the police station first to set up a search team. It should only take an hour. Then we can question Christina and Bradford. They aren't going anywhere." Hawk suggested.

"A search team—that's a good idea, Hawk."

"I can talk to Ray, the police chief. I used to work for him. If anyone could help us put together a search team, it would be him."

Justin agreed.

***

When they arrived at the police station, they saw chaos everywhere. Uniformed police officers ran around, answering phones, and trying to keep control of looters. Hawk waved to Ray, who was talking on the phone in his office.

Ray motioned for Hawk and Justin to come inside.

Hawk introduced Justin and explained the story about Ashley's disappearance. "We need to fill out a missing person report." Hawk said.

"I'll get you the paperwork." Ray said.

Justin interrupted. "Is it possible to set up a search team?"

"Our phones are ringing off the hooks with calls about missing persons. But I'll see what I can do to get a search team set up for Ashley. Let me get some information." Ray said as he handed Justin the paperwork.

Justin sat down for about an hour filling out paperwork and giving Ray the details about Ashley.

After they had set up the search team, Justin went over to Ashley's parent's house to update them, and see if they wanted to join the team to search for Ashley.

***

Justin pulled up to Ashley's parent's home late in the afternoon. He looked around and saw debris scattered throughout their neighborhood, but it wasn't as bad as downtown.   He saw them standing on the porch when he pulled up to the curb. Ashley's mother ran up to him.

"Have you found out anything?" she asked in a frantic voice.

"No, I haven't. But I set up a search team at the Police Station."

"A search team.   Oh my God."   Cynthia clutched her heart. "I hope my baby is not dead?"

"Come on Mrs. Jacobs. Let's go inside." Justin said in a sympathetic voice. He held his arm around her shoulder as they walked toward the house. "You coming Mr. Jacobs?"

Ashley's father said nothing. He followed them inside the house.

Once inside, Justin told them about Ashley's handbag, cell phone and the wine glasses.

"Where could she have gone?" Her mother said.

"I have the search team and my private investigator looking for Ashley. We'll find her." Justin said, staring at Mr. Jacobs pacing the floor in the living room.

"It looks like a bomb went off outside. We have to find my daughter." Daniel said with a glazed look in his eyes. The earthquake had brought back memories of Desert Storm.

Cynthia rolled her eyes and whispered in Justin's ear. "He's been like this since the earthquake hit. He thinks a bomb went off, and that he is back in Desert Storm."

"I'm okay as long as he doesn't hurt you Mrs. Jacobs." Justin said under his breath.

"What was that you said?" David said staring at Justin.

Justin ignored Daniel's outburst and talked to Cynthia. "I'm going to continue to look for Ashley after I leave here. Do you both want to join the search team to look for Ashley?"

"Yes. We'll drive down to the police station right now." Cynthia said.

"Good. I'll meet you both there. Don't worry we'll find Ashley. But before I go, I'd like to have a word with you both."

They all sat at the dining room table. Justin stared at the redwood tree as he spoke. "Ashley told me about your PTSD, Mr. Jacobs."

"Yeah. They gave me some medicine at the V.A. for my condition, but I don't like the way it makes me feel."

Crossing his arms, Justin pressed his lips together. He wanted to convince Mr. Jacobs to gain control of his PTSD. "Mr. Jacobs, you need to change your prescription or request for some other help from the V.A. for your own safety. I cannot allow you to terrorize Ashley or her mother anymore. You are a victim as much as they."

David stared at the redwood tree while he listened to Justin's words. He'd wanted to change, for years, but couldn't help himself. Somehow, Ashley's disappearance and Justin's ultimatum brought him out of his self-destructive mentality. "I'll get my prescription changed or get some therapy for my condition." With glistening eyes, he looked at Justin. "I can't lose Ashley. I already lost my son. I don't like going through my episodes, and I don't like hurting my family." He confessed.

"Good. Mr. Jacobs. I'll help you if you want." Justin stood up. "I'll meet you both down at the police station."

Ashley took a deep breath of stale air and continued to chip away at the concrete with the crowbar. She saw that the flashlight was going dim.

Barely able to breathe, she took a sip of her water and then looked at her wrist watch. It was after six o'clock. She'd been stuck in there for over five hours.

Her only thought was getting out from under the pile of concrete. She wiped away beads of sweat rolling down her face. She continued to chip away at the concrete, even though, the job was moving slowly. The muscles in her arms were beginning to sting. She began to feel fatigue. She was running out of energy. She stopped for a moment and sat still.

She said a prayer. "Please give me the grace and strength to get out of here safely." Suddenly her second wind came. She continued to chip away at the concrete while honking her horn now and then.

Chapter 17

Early Monday morning Justin drove over to Christina's house where he'd planned to meet Hawk. On the way there, he saw a fire truck and several firefighters digging through an old overpass that had crumbled into a concrete heap. Something made him stop in the middle of the road. He listened to his gut feeling and began to think. Could Ashley be under that rubble? Maybe she was on her way over to Christina's house when the earthquake hit. It was a long shot, but he had to take a stab at the possibility. Suddenly stark fear crossed Justin's face. How could Ashley possibly survive under all that rubble? Whoever was under there was probably dead, he thought. He walked up to the firefighters.

"Is there someone stuck under all of that concrete?"

One firefighter turned around with sweat dripping from his face. "Yes. There is someone under the concrete. We heard a horn honking a minute ago. Cal-Trans workers are on the way to help remove the debris."

"Could that be Ashley?" Justin said out loud.

"What?" the firefighter asked.

"I was just wondering. My girlfriend is missing.

I wonder if that could be her honking her horn."

"Whoever it is, they will not be getting out anytime soon. But we do know that they are alive right now. It might take days to dig them out."

"Can I help? It could be my girlfriend?"

"No. You'll just be in the way. Wait until the Cal-Trans construction crew removes some of the debris and then come back."

"Okay. I'll come back in an hour."

The firefighter kept digging.

Justin reached Christina's house and didn't see Hawk's car. He waited until Hawk arrived. They both knocked on Christina's door. Bradford answered the door bare chested, wearing boxer shorts.

"Christina here?" Justin asked, getting straight to the point. Justin looked rough because he hadn't slept well or shaved in two days.

"No. She left for work about an hour ago." Bradford's eyes widened when he saw Hawk. He remembered him taking photos at the restaurant.

"When was the last time you saw Ashley?" Justin questioned. He wanted to find out if they were over at Ashley's house and if they had anything to do with her disappearance.

"The last time I saw Ashley was yesterday when we had lunch with her." He paused with a dry mouth. "Christina wanted to leave right after we arrived."

"Why did she want to leave so fast?" Justin asked.

"I don't know." Bradford hunched his shoulders. "When I came out of the restroom, Christina was ready to go." Bradford looked away.

"You and Christina were the last two people to see Ashley yesterday. Where did Ashley go?" Justin asked.

"I don't know." Fear, stark and vivid, flickered in Bradford's eyes.

Hawk nudged Justin to stop. He believed Bradford was telling the truth.

"Can we come inside?" Justin asked.

Bradford blocked the entrance.

Hawk stepped forward pushing his way through the door. "Move out the way."

Justin followed behind Hawk, looking around the apartment. They all sat down at the kitchen table.

"Want a beer?" Bradford offered to stall for time to think.

"This ain't no social visit!" Hawk barked.

"You have anything to do with Ashley's lawsuit?" Justin asked in a cool voice.

"Lawsuit? No. I had nothing to do with that," Bradford lied.

Justin took his cell phone and photos out of his jacket pocket. "I want you to take a look at these photos and this video, and rethink your answer." He said pressing the play button on the video.

Bradford stood up and pushed back his chair. "Sit down," Hawk said, standing up and pushing Bradford back down.

Justin spread the photos out evenly on the table as the video played. "Now, I'll ask you one more time. Did you have anything to do with Ashley's lawsuit?" Justin asked as he pressed the record button on his cell phone to record Bradford's response.

"Okay, okay. Kimberly faked a neck injury and filed a lawsuit against the spa. All three of us planned to split the $250,000 from Ashley's insurance company."

"Why did you do it?" Justin asked.

"Because I need the money to pay for my daughter's heart surgery. She has a hole in her heart."

JANICE L. DENNIE

Justin's brows drew closer, his jaw tightened. He could spot a liar a mile away, but Bradford's body language didn't lie. Justin believed Bradford wasn't lying about his daughter. "What about Christina and Kimberly? Why did they do it?

"Kimberly's brother just got out of prison. He showed her how to get money out of Ashley's insurance company." Bradford said throwing Christina and Kimberly under the bus.

"What about Christina?"

"Christina hates Ashley. She told me she's hated Ashley since they were kids."

"Humph." Justin knew he was right about Christina. She was no friend of Ashley. His gut never lied.

***

Justin and Hawk drove over to the spa and confronted Christina in the massage room folding towels.

"We just spoke with Bradford. He said that you both were at Ashley's house yesterday."

"Yeah. He's right. We were supposed to have lunch, but all we had was a glass of wine."

"Do you know where Ashley went after you and Bradford left? Justin asked.

"No. I don't," she said folding a towel.

"But you saw the photos on Ashley's coffee table."

"Yeah. I saw them," she said throwing a towel into a basket.

"Bradford admitted that you, he and Kimberly were all behind Ashley's lawsuit. Is that true?"

Christina slowly lifted her head, bracing her hands on the laundry basket. She gave Justin a hostile glare.

His question triggered her memory back to the day she'd deliberately kicked Ashley's insurance bill under the receptionist's desk. She, Bradford and Kimberly had come up with the idea of filing a fraudulent lawsuit against the spa. Originally, Ashley's insurance company was supposed to pay for the damages, but Christina made sure that Kimberly's injury happened after Ashley's insurance had lapsed. That way Ashley would have to pay for the damages out of her pocket. She wanted Ashley to suffer financially, the way she'd suffered all of her life.

But now that Justin was asking all of these questions, she knew she was busted. She placed a neatly folded towel in the laundry basket. She couldn't see any way of getting out of this, so she confessed. Slamming the laundry basket on the floor, she met Justin's accusing eyes with a hostile glare. "Yeah. Bradford's right. I helped plot the lawsuit because, I hate Ashley. And yes, I hid her insurance bill, hoping it would lapse." She threw her words at him like stones. "I wanted to get Ashley where it hurts—in her bank account."

Justin's eyes were as hard as black granite. He felt nothing but contempt for Christina's betrayal and hypocrisy. "You tell your friend Kimberly that she can drop the lawsuit, or all three of you will face prison time. You and Bradford know from those photos and the video that I have enough evidence to prove insurance fraud."

Christina took heed to Justin's threat. Lowering her head, she hung her arms to her sides in defeat. "We'll drop it."

Justin's lip curled. "Ashley's loyalty to you has blinded her to your true character. But I can see through you like glass. I know that you are not and never have been Ashley's friend!"

Christina's eyes narrowed as she watched Justin walk out.

Chapter 18

It was Wednesday. Ashley had been missing for four days. Justin had walked all over the city, with the search team and Ashley's parents looking for Ashley. Every day, Justin drove over to the overpass. The Cal-Trans construction crew had made great headway removing the concrete. Justin asked a construction worker a question.

"Have you heard any voices or anything other than the honking horn?"

"I haven't heard any voices yet."

Justin walked up to the remaining concrete and yelled at the top of his voice. "Ashley! Are you in there? Can you hear me?" Justin could have sworn he heard a faint voice cry out his name. "Ashley! Is that you?" He began to pull pieces of concrete away with his bare hands.

"Sorry, sir. That is dangerous. For your own safety, I can't allow you to help."

Justin ignored the worker. "Ashley. Is that you?" He heard the faint voice again. Then he heard the car horn honk. He had a gut feeling that Ashley was in there. "Honk your horn three times if that's you Ashley," Justin yelled. The horn honked three times. He fell on his knees relieved that he'd found Ashley. He thanked God for answering his prayer. He began calling out her name over and over. "Ashley…Ashley…I'll get you out, Baby. Just hold on!"

Ashley sat in the car, ashen, dehydrated and weak for lack of water. She was just about to give up when she'd heard a faint voice call out her name. It was Justin. She perked up and called out his name over and over. "Justin… Justin." After she'd honked her horn, she leaned over the steering wheel and began to cry. She'd thought she was going to die. She'd never been so happy to hear Justin's voice until now.

After hearing Justin's voice, Ashley realized how much she loved him. The only thought that crossed her mind was how much of a fool she'd been to treat him so badly over those photos. Tears slid down her cheeks as she thought about Justin. All she wanted was to be held in his arms once again. She wanted to apologize and let him know how much she loved him. After hearing his voice, she mustered enough strength to continue chipping away at the concrete until she made a small opening. Now she could see daylight. She yelled out as loud as she could. "Justin!"

***

Justin ran toward Ashley's voice and saw the small hole. "I hear you, Baby! I'll get you out of there. Hurry up!" he said to the exhausted Cal-Trans construction workers.

"For your own safety sir, you need to step back."

"Are you married?" Justin asked.

"Yes, I am."

Imagine that your wife was under there. Would you simply step away for your own safety?

"No.   I wouldn't" He understood Justin's urgency.

"Okay." He looked around. "You can help."

Justin peeped through the small hole and saw Ashley's eye looking back at him. "It's me, Baby. How do you feel?"

"I'm real weak, Justin.   There's no air; I can barely breathe."

"Put your nose up to the hole to get some fresh air."

Ashley leaned over the car door window and put her nostril near the hole. Justin picked debris away from the hole to make it a little larger. He kept picking away at the debris with bloody fingers, until he could see Ashley's face.

Ashley began coughing. "I'm stuck in my car. I can't get the door open."

Justin turned to the construction worker. "I'll

pay you a bonus if you can get her out of there today. You name the price."

"We can't take your money, sir, but we'll do everything we can to get her out ASAP."

Justin stared at him, pacing back and forth.

The Cal-Trans construction worker texted more of his crew on his cell phone. Within thirty minutes, there was a team of burly men removing debris from the underpass. An hour later, they had made great progress. Justin could see Ashley through the window of her car. She was leaning back against the front seat covered with gray concrete dust.

"Bottled water. Anybody got a bottle of water?"

One of the construction workers took a bottle out of his lunch pail and handed it to Justin. Justin opened it and poured it on Ashley's face.

She began coughing. "Hurry up and get her out of there."

The men worked frantically to remove the debris surrounding the car door. After they cleared enough debris, Justin opened the car door. "Ashley...Ashley." She didn't respond. She'd passed out from sheer exhaustion.

A firefighter came up to Justin. "Stand aside sir

and let me get her out."

The firefighter removed Ashley from the car and placed her onto a gurney. The EMT ambulance driver immediately placed an oxygen mask over her face and rolled her in the ambulance.

Justin jumped into the ambulance. "I'm going with her to the hospital."

***

Several hours had passed, and a tall, young doctor with a kind face came out and asked Justin and Ashley's parents if they were Ashley's family. They all nodded. "She's dehydrated and weak. All she needs now is rest and fluids."

"When can I see her?" Justin asked.

The doctor said. "She won't be awake until tomorrow. Why don't you go home and get some rest and come back tomorrow."

"No way! I can't go home." Justin dismissed the doctor's words. An unspoken pain glowed in Justin's eyes as he realized what had happened. Ashley was on her way to Christina's house when the earthquake hit and trapped her under that underpass.

Justin spent the night in the hospital after her parents left. Before falling asleep in a chair, he walked over to Ashley and looked down at her face and hair still covered in remnants of concrete dust. Her lips were cracked, her complexion sallow. He said a prayer before going to sleep. He didn't leave her bedside until the next morning.

Chapter 19

Justin opened the hospital door slowly and walked inside. He'd taken a quick trip to the men's room to wash up. He walked over to the window and opened the blinds to illuminate the room with natural sunlight. He didn't want Ashley to wake up to a dark, sterile room. He leaned over to get a closer look at her face again. His eyes softened when he saw that her normal complexion had returned. She no longer had that sickly complexion she had last night. She looked beautiful to Justin, even with the concrete dust in her hair.

Looking at Ashley's face in the light of day made Justin feel happy. He began walking around the room unable to sit still. He stuck his head through the door and instructed the nurse to get the doctor. He looked at her face once again, wishing she would wake up. The doctor entered the room wearing his white coat and carrying Ashley's chart. Another doctor had come in to check on Ashley several times through the night.

Justin dug his hands into his back pockets and moved away from Ashley to give the doctor some room. He looked into the doctor's eyes. "Looks like her color has returned. Is she still dehydrated?"

The doctor stood above Ashley. "Yes. I see her color is good." He raised one of Ashley's eyelids and took some vitals and then took another look at her chart. With the return of her complexion, he thought she would wake up at any moment. "I just want to monitor her kidneys."

Justin sat in a chair, holding his head in the palms of his hands. He was relieved to hear the doctor's report and felt grateful that Ashley had survived.

He walked over to the doctor and shook his hand. "Thank you for saving her life." He exhaled deeply releasing bent up tension he'd been holding since Ashley had been admitted. "What can I do?"

"Let the nurse know when she wakes up. She'll be hungry and thirsty. The nurse can bring in something for her to drink and eat."

"When can she leave?"

"Maybe tomorrow if her kidneys are functioning properly." The doctor left the room.

Justin pulled out his cell phone and called Henrietta. "Hi, Granny. Ashley survived. She is recovering."

"I've been praying for her all night," Henrietta said.

"Thank you, Granny. I feel like I'm floating on air."

Suddenly Ashley's eyes fluttered opened. "Tell your grandmother I said hello," she said in a dry voice.

Justin turned his head around and saw Ashley staring back at him. "She's awake, Granny. I'll talk to you later."

Justin walked over to Ashley and took her hand, kissing it softly. "I was worried about you, Sweetness."

Ashley spoke through dry, cracked lips, "I feel like I've been hit by a train."

Justin bent down and kissed her cheek, still holding her hand. "Let me get your nurse."

"Thanks. My throat is dry, and I'm starving."

Justin ran out to get the nurse. She came back with a pitcher of water and breakfast. She helped Ashley sit up as Justin watched. Justin sat down in the chair next to Ashley's bed and hand fed her.

"How long do I have to stay here?" Ashley asked, taking in a spoonful of oatmeal. "I can feed myself," She said taking the spoon from Justin.

Justin smiled. "The doctor wants to monitor your kidneys. He thinks you can go home tomorrow."

Ashley sipped some water through a straw in a

plastic cup and finished her breakfast. "How long have I been here?"

"Since yesterday."

"The last thing I remember was talking to you and breathing through that little hole and then I blacked out."

After the nurse had left, Justin stood up. "When I saw you unconscious in the car, I was never so afraid in my life."

"Before I passed out, all I could think about was apologizing to you, Justin. I realized that I was blind. I'm sorry for treating you so badly. I should have listened to you when you showed me those photos. I knew you were telling the truth about Christina, but I was in denial. One thing about being in denial is that you tend to ignore facts staring you in the face. Can you ever forgive me?"

"Baby, I already have. Don't even think about those photos. All I want is for you to get well and please tell me that you still love me and will marry me."

"Marry you?"

"Yes. I'm asking you right now. I'll get on one knee if you want."

Ashley looked into his eyes. "Justin, you are the only man in this world for me. Yes. I will marry you. Being stuck in that car for so long made me think about a lot of things. Not knowing if I was going to live or die made me face some harsh realities. Keeping my peace of mind at all costs is no longer an option. My head is officially out of the clouds. I'm no longer afraid to face conflict. Like you said, it is a part of life. All I want now Justin, is to spend the rest of my life with you."

Justin leaned over her and kissed her forehead. "That's all I wanted to hear." Then his mind turned to what started all of this in the first place. He stood over her staring her in the eye. "Where were you going when you got stuck in that underpass?"

"I was on my way to Christina's house. I wanted to hear her admit out of her own mouth why she'd betrayed me. When I was stuck in that car, I not only thought of my weaknesses, but I had a lot of time to think about the meaning of friendship. Friendship means to love our friends as we love ourselves. It hurt me to my core, to accept the fact that Christina never cared about me as a friend. I'm curious to find out why she carried on the charade all these years."

"I wouldn't give Christina a second thought, if I were you," Justin said explaining how Christina, Bradford and Kimberly had dropped the lawsuit.

***

One week later, Ashley drove up to the spa. Christina was in the massage room. She'd just finished with a customer when Ashley walked in and closed the door.

Christina's eyes widened. She'd stayed at the spa even though she'd been pegged as the perpetrator of Ashley's fraudulent lawsuit because she hoped Ashley would do as she'd always done. Forgive and forget, and move on with life.

"Christina, I have one question. Why did you betray me?"

"What do you mean?" Christina began to fold a sheet.

"I'll ask you again. Why?"

Christina could feel that Ashley was no longer in denial, so she confessed. "You want to know why? I'll tell you why, Miss Ashley. You've always had everything. You have beauty, money, a successful business and what do I have? Nothing!"

"That's not true Christina. You have good looks. You have marketable skills. You could have started your own business. You earn good money at the spa."

"Money? Are you kidding? I don't live off my grandfather's trust fund like you."

Now that Ashley had heard Christina's reasons from her own mouth, she frowned. "You're jealous," Ashley stated angrily. "There's more to life than money. What about honesty and trust. Those are two things you know nothing about."

"So you're not going to forgive me?"

"Sure. I'll forgive you Christina. I'll also forgive Bradford."

Christina smiled. "We dropped the lawsuit."

"I just have one thing to say to you, Christina."

"What's that?" Christina asked as she continued to fold the sheet.

"You're fired. Bradford, too. I should've never taken your recommendation to hire him. I hope everything goes well for his daughter's surgery. All he had to do was ask, and I would have tried to help him. He didn't have to plot against me."

Christina stared at Ashley with her mouth half open in disbelief. For all these years, she'd taken Ashley's friendship for granted. But now, Ashley had changed. She was confrontational and clearly unafraid to face her enemies.

Chapter 20

Justin and Ashley were married in June, the following year, at the Underwood Hills Winery. Chairs painted a soft gold filled the areas on both sides of the aisle.

Justin wore a black tuxedo with mint accessories as he stood with Kenton standing in as his best man.

Kenton watched Justin fidgeting with his cummerbund. He patted him on the back. "Don't be nervous, Brother. You'll be glad you married Ashley. I don't know how I ever lived without Briana." Kenton said, winking at Briana, who was holding Jonathan, their baby boy.

"I'm okay. I guess Carter will be next." Justin replied.

"I guess so, because I can't imagine anyone wanting to marry Brandon," Kenton said.

"I agree." They both laughed.

Reverend J. L. Brown, Henrietta's minister from her church, presided over the wedding, holding his bible.

Justin had talked Ashley's father into getting some post-traumatic stress disorder treatment from the VA. He and his wife, along with their friends and family sat quietly on the bride's side of the aisle. Henrietta sat in her wheelchair in the front row. Justin's mother and his siblings along with family and friends filled up the groom's side.

Justin straightened up when he heard the sound of a harp playing the wedding march. A little girl led the procession wearing a soft mint dress, white frilly socks and white patent leather Mary Jane's. Ashley's sister Melissa was the maid of honor. She followed wearing a mint organza gown. Then, everyone stood up as Justin's beautiful bride walked down the aisle. Ashley wore a slim Chantilly lace v-neckline gown designed with flowers and ribbons on an organza background. She carried a bouquet of blush colored roses. Guests stood up and whispered at her sweeping train and low back dress.

When Ashley reached the dais, Justin looked into her eyes and never looked away. After the minister had finished reciting the vows, Justin and Ashley kissed.

Henrietta wiped away her tears with an embroidered handkerchief and whispered, "Two down, three to go."

THE END

JANICE L. DENNIE

About The Author

Janice L. Dennie began her writing career in 1997 with her debut novel, *The Lion of Judah*. Her second book, *Moon Goddess Queen of Sheba*, was published in August 1999.

Kenton's Vintage Affair her first book in *The Underwood's of Napa Valley* series, introduced readers to the fictitious Underwood family, owners of a successful winery in Napa Valley. *Justin's Body of Work*, book 2 in The Underwood's of Napa Valley series, introduces the reader to Justin, the second brother in the family.

Janice was born in Denver, Colorado and raised in Northern California. After graduating from college, Janice began working for a federal agency as a computer systems analyst and contracting officer. She services her community through various charities and non-profits. Currently, she writes full-time and lives in Northern California with her family.

To read more about Janice, visit her website at:
http://www.janicedennie.com

www.ingramcontent.com/pod-product-compliance
Lightning Source LLC
Chambersburg PA
CBHW021104130626
46554CB00002B/527